MW01613296

THE GENTILE APOSTLE

By

Dorothy Frisby

Copyright © 2007 by Dorothy Frisby

The Gentile Apostle
by Dorothy Frisby

Printed in the United States of America

ISBN 978-1-60266-475-3

All rights reserved solely by the author. The author guarantees all contents are original and do not infringe upon the legal rights of any other person or work. No part of this book may be reproduced in any form without the permission of the author. The views expressed in this book are not necessarily those of the publisher.

Unless otherwise indicated, Bible quotations are taken from The New American Bible. Copyright © 1987 by Devore and Sons, Inc. Wichita, Kansas 67201

www.xulonpress.com

To Ron,

May our Risen Lord bless you abundantly every day of your life.

Dorothy Frisby

Table of Contents

On The Island Of Patmos 7

Experience at Cana 13

Meeting John the Baptist 19

Witnessing Healing Miracles 25

Healing Longinus' Servant 33

The Arrest of Jesus 37

Jesus' Suffering and Death 45

The Resurrection 59

Meeting With Peter 67

The Ascension 79

The Descent of the Holy Spirit 87

Proclaiming the Covenant 97

Paul and Luke 109

Mary's Farewell 123

Mark and John 141

On the Island of Patmos

I am now an old man, sitting and trying to warm my old bones in the summer sun. My benefactor and companion is also old and ill, but seems driven to complete letters he is writing to seven of the established churches in the region. He is John, just a little younger than I, and one of the dearest disciples of our Master, Jesus.

This island of Patmos has been our home for some years now, when the Romans sent us here as exiles. We live in a cave about halfway up the largest hill, and have made it as comfortable as possible. We were allowed to bring enough servants so that we can live without too many problems. They have planted olive trees, vineyards, and a large vegetable garden, besides raising sheep and goats for our meals. We rely heavily on their catching fish, which is one of the main staples of our diet. Life is simple here and very quiet, and we are looking forward to the day when we will be allowed to leave. Rulers come and go, empires rise and fall, and we trust that with change, we will once again be free men.

John has urged me to write my own story, so people who come after us will know more about the man we both served, who was so much more than just a man. This is the teacher known as Jesus of Nazareth, who selected his inner group of apostles with great care. It is the story of how Jesus also selected me to be his first Gentile Apostle, and how drastically my life changed after I had several encounters with him.

My name used to be Marcus Antonius Silvanus when I was a Roman citizen and a soldier. Since the reign of the Emperor Tiberius, I have been known as Mark bar Matthias, a Jew from the region of Capernaum. I was born into a wealthy family in Rome, two years before the death of Augustus Caesar, and spent the first years of my life being educated there. My mother died when I was still a young boy, and my father decided to move away from Rome after her passing. My father was a merchant and had a warehouse in Rome. He left one of his brothers in charge of that, and he and I, with a houseful of slaves, moved to Joppa in Palestine. Father established a business there, dealing with silks, spices, and many other things which came from the Silk Route, the desert, and other exotic places. He would purchase in bulk and ship the merchandise from Joppa to Rome, where his brother would put the items in markets and sell at a good profit.

When we lived in Palestine, I had only neighbor boys to play with. As a result, I learned to speak Aramaic as well as any Jew. I had been taught both

Latin and Greek, and even picked up some Hebrew phrases from my Jewish playmates. Spending so much time out in the sun darkened my skin and toughened my body. The only problem I encountered with this was when any of the Roman soldiers rode through our town. Generally, they were fairly indifferent to the people whose country they occupied in the name of the emperor. Occasionally, though, one or a group of soldiers seemed to be full of hatred and spite, and often took out their rage on any hapless person that crossed their path. They saw me as just another Hebrew boy, and I sometimes suffered the same ridicule and punishments that they meted out to all the Jews.

My father wanted me to enter the political arena and become a Senator in Rome. One of the speediest ways to do this was to join the Roman army and serve for a 10 year period. After being released from the army, it was a simple matter for a wealthy person to rise very fast, especially if he was really an ambitious sort. Therefore, when I reached the age of eighteen, my father encouraged me to join the army. I went to Rome for a few months for training and indoctrination, then was shipped back to Palestine. My knowledge of the language and customs of these people were thought to be valuable assets.

Thus, my life as a Roman soldier began. Since I knew so many languages, and could read and write, I was expected to serve directly under the centurion in charge as an aide and scribe. I was also expected to fight in any battles, and experienced my share of skirmishes and battles. The Roman army was truly formidable. Under the tutelage of Julius Caesar many years before, the training generated an unstoppable force of men. I saw my share of fighting and killing, and quickly learned how to blend into this effective powerhouse.

When Tiberius was in about his 20th year as emperor, a new army of soldiers was sent to Palestine, under the centurion Longinus Proctus. I was assigned to him as his aide and scribe, and served him for the rest of my time as a soldier.

Longinus was in his mid 30s and very handsome. He was somewhat taller than the average man, so he stood out in any crowd. His skin was weathered and leathery from years of exposure, but his hair was dark gold in color. This contrasted strikingly with his dark brown eyebrows and brown eyes. He was well built and worked out daily with his weapons to stay in prime condition. He was a man of great self-discipline, and he loved reading and discussing philosophy, which he had learned while stationed in Greece. He and I quickly became friends as well as officer and subordinate, and spent many evenings discussing many topics. He had an astute mind, and a quick grasp of problems that would arise, combined with a sense of justice and fairness. He looked at the Jewish people as human beings instead of simply as rabble-rousing troublemakers, as most of the Romans did. Knowing my educational background, Longinus often called me to his quarters simply to relax and debate various issues with me.

My life was well organized and planned, and the days passed mostly uneventfully. With this background, hopefully the reader will follow me as I meet various men and women, and understand the changes that I had to undergo after meeting some of these people. The most remarkable man is the one that I had the least physical contact with, but who had the greatest impact on my life. This story is about my few chance meetings with the man called Jesus, the Rabbi from Nazareth, and how my life was altered forever and always.

Experience at Cana

The first encounter with Jesus that I remember was at a wedding celebration. Often during our occupation of this country, we had to travel to various locations to put down disturbances caused by the inhabitants. It seemed that they were always plotting to overthrow us and expel us from their country, although no power on earth had yet been able to do so.

On one occasion, we were sent out from our base to quell yet another insurrection in the hills outside Sepphoris. There were only 20 legionaries with our centurion, Longinus, to guide us. We knew that a ragged band of outlaws would be no match for our highly trained and heavily armed group.

We were getting hungry as we were passing through a little town called Cana. It was somewhat west and south of our destination, and we heard sounds of revelry coming from one of the houses on the outskirts of the village. Longinus decided to pause there for lunch, ordering the household slaves to serve all of us. Two young female slaves then began to move back and forth from the kitchen to the shaded courtyard where we rested. They brought food from the wedding feast that was the cause of all the noise we had heard. They served us wine and we rested and enjoyed the local food, even though it wasn't comparable to the cuisine served in Rome.

We finished eating, and Longinus called for more wine. A pretty, innocent looking slave, who told us her name was Dorcas, came toward him with her eyes lowered and with a trembling voice, told him, "I am sorry, Master, but they have just run out of wine inside." Longinus did not believe her, and gave her a slap on the behind. She ran back into the house in tears. Longinus growled, "When have you ever heard of one of these Jewish feasts running out of wine, especially at a wedding celebration?" Together, we stared at the retreating form of Dorcas.

As she reached the portico, we noticed a flurry of activity there. Several servants were busily filling water jars that stood at the side of the portico. Behind them, we could see the form of a man, but he stood in shadows, and we could see only that part of him that was in the sunlight, which was from about the waist down. He seemed to be watching while the servants filled the water jars. They finally stepped back and looked toward him. He moved forward so that just his head was in the shadows, and he stretched out his hands over the water jugs. Then he said something to one of the slaves and turned and went back into the house. The slave drew some water out of the jug and went into the house as well.

Longinus in the meantime had worked himself up into a fury at the impertinence of the slave refusing us wine. He said, "These Jews all seem to think they don't need to give us any respect. Well, I will just have to show them who is master here." And he began to stride toward the house.

As he reached the door, two more female slaves appeared behind Dorcas, and they were carrying trays with wine cups toward us. "See," Longinus bellowed, "I knew all along that they just didn't want to share with us." "Nay, Master," Dorcas said. Her eyes were as big as a startled fawn's, and she appeared to be in a highly excited state. "This is but water." Longinus sipped from the cup and slapped his thigh. "Hah!" he shouted. "This is not water, but simply the best wine I have ever tasted. It is even superior to what we have in Rome. Now, tell me, sweet Dorcas, exactly where you have been hiding this, and where we can get more."

Dorcas began by looking straight into Longinus' eyes, which was practically forbidden for any slave to do. She drew herself up and began to tell us her version of what happened.

"We did run out of wine, and there is no mistake about that at all. One of the ladies who was there with her son and some of their friends noticed that we had emptied all the wine jars. She went to her son and talked with him for awhile, and it appeared that she was asking him to do something, but he didn't agree with her. Soon, she came to us and told us that whatever he asked us to do, that we should do it without question."

"After a few moments, the man, her son, came to us and told us to fill all the jars with water from the well. This we did, and told him when they were full. He stood there for a little while with his eyes partially closed, and then he told us to draw out some of the water and bring it to the wine steward. Again, we followed his orders, but when we drew the water from the jar, it looked like wine. We were all shocked, but I personally took a cup to the wine steward, and he exclaimed that it was the best wine we had served all day. I am telling you the truth, sir," Dorcas insisted. "Tell me, what is the name of this man?" Longinus asked. Dorcas replied, "His mother's name is Mary, the widow of Joseph the carpenter from Nazareth. Her son's name is Jesus." Longinus seemed to file this name away in his memory for future reference, and then said, "Well, no matter, just bring us some more of this wonderful nectar before we continue our journey."

All of us truly enjoyed this remarkable wine, and I was struck by the story. It seemed too fantastic to be true, yet the story told by Dorcas had the ring of sincerity. Everyone knows that you cannot fill a jar with water and have delicious wine come out of it. Yet, this is precisely what Dorcas said she personally witnessed, and reported to us exactly as it happened. I pondered deeply in my heart how this could be, and I also kept it in my mind as we marched toward Sepphoris. Leaving the peaceful courtyard, I could see many of the wedding guests moving around inside, and I watched them, wondering which one had done this incredible thing. For some strange reason, I seemed to feel a tugging somewhere deep within my being. I actually had to fight the desire to run into the house to see this Jesus. As we moved further away from the wedding festivities, this desire faded until I no longer had to struggle with it.

Meeting John the Baptist

Herod had sent for help from the Roman military once again. It seemed that a holy man whom the Jewish people considered a great prophet had gained notoriety with his preaching along the Jordan River. These Zealots were constantly plotting for the overthrow of Herod, the Romans, in fact, all types of authority. Many thought this man might be one of these insurgents, and was attempting to gain a large enough following to accomplish all these things. Consequently, our troop began the march southeast of Jericho, to the banks of the Jordan River where this man usually talked to the countless hordes of people who swarmed there to listen.

We learned that his name was simply "John," and his father had been a priest in the temple. Stories about him ran rampant through the land. One was that his mother had been a very old woman when she conceived him, which we all knew was impossible. Another was that his father had been visited by an angel who foretold his birth. We all laughed at these stories, as yet another example of the stupidity and gullibility of these people whom we worked so hard to keep under control. Yet, having been so closely associated with them when I was a boy, I couldn't help but feel that there was more to these stories than simply fiction.

We were ordered to spend one to two weeks there simply observing, unless we saw signs of rebellion. We marched along the banks of the Jordan River. In some places it was marshy, but mostly the river wound serenely along a winding path through shaded banks. Trees and bushes grew lushly along either side of the river, and in some places we passed rapids, where the ground dropped and there were rocks in the riverbed which caused small waterfalls to occur. The sound of the bubbling water rushing over the rocks was soothing, and as we walked along, were all lulled into a kind of waking sleep.

Soon we arrived at a bend in the river, where there had been a flood and now was a backwater. There was a high promontory above this area, and we arranged ourselves on this high ground, to be seen by the people. Mostly our presence alone kept the mobs under control. We could see a circular pool beneath the cliff on which we stood, which obviously had been formed by past flooding of the Jordan River. There was a large group of people standing on the bank of this pool, and they seemed to have formed a line from the edge of the pool to a man standing waist deep just under where our troop was standing. The man looked almost like a wild man, clothed in animal hides, and with a long, unkempt beard and unruly hair.

We could hear this man as he spoke. He kept up a constant stream of what seemed to us babbling. He was continuously calling for the people to "Repent, for the kingdom of God is at hand." We could not hear anything that sounded seditious or against Roman rule, but we kept our ears open nonetheless. The man, and we determined that this was indeed John, the Baptist, as he had become known, was simply preaching goodness and love for one another, and seemed especially to dwell on the sinfulness of man. He took each person that came to him and held him as he immersed him in the pool. As the person came out of the water, John would tell him or her that their sins were forgiven, and that they should go and live good lives without sin from now on, awaiting the kingdom of God, which was imminent.

We spent several days in this area, watching for any sign of danger. Each day many of us remained at the base camp, but many more scouts were sent out to look in nearby areas for the rebellious Zealots that you could find all over this country. They usually formed in groups and stayed in the wilderness plotting their actions. Many of them supported themselves by preying on travelers going through the area. They would descend upon the travelers and rob them, sometimes openly and sometimes in secret, waiting for people to sleep at night. Then they would slink into the traveler's camps and take what they could without anyone knowing. In a few cases, people had been badly wounded or sometimes even killed, and this could not be allowed. Rome prided herself on keeping peace in all her conquered countries.

Days passed while I stood and watched John preaching. He continuously exhorted his listeners to change their lives, to prepare for the coming of the Messiah, and to repent of all their evil ways. This repetitious preaching became very monotonous, and we began to feel drowsy in the afternoon sun. Even though there were numerous trees and shade where we were standing, the warmth permeated our being and we all began to feel sleepy. Suddenly, though, I sensed something different in the air. It was almost as though everything around me had ceased to move, and was frozen in place. There was also a hush as all the birds stopped singing, and I felt the hairs on my head and body begin to rise. It felt like the sensation I had once when I was much younger and was in close proximity to a lightning bolt. The earth beneath my feet seemed to tremble very slightly, as a human would tremble with excitement.

I looked over to the crowd that was still standing in line, and noticed one lone figure. He stood apart from everyone and seemed deep in thought. For some inexplicable reason, my gaze was drawn to him, and I could not seem to take my eyes from him. He seemed to be deep in thought, and his lips moved slightly as if he were talking to someone. There was a strange glow surrounding him which seemed to come from the sun, yet the light was shining only on him. Soon, all the people had been immersed in the water by John, and there was a pause. The man I had been watching then began to wade out into the pool toward John, and he was staring straight into John's eyes. John himself seemed almost poised to bolt like a startled deer, as he watched the man walking toward him. As they came together, I could hear their voices. I heard John say, "Surely it is you who should be baptizing me." The other man looked deeply into John's eyes and said, "Let it be thus for now. It is fitting."

John then took hold of the man and immersed him in water, saying the same prayers that he had said for all the other people. Everyone seemed to be electrified, watching this panoply enacted. When the man emerged from the water, there was a gasp from the crowd. As I watched, I too saw it. A beam of light came from the sky and played around the head and shoulders of the man. Suddenly there was a pure white dove hovering over him as well. I heard a low rumbling, as of thunder. Others claimed to have heard an actual voice claiming that, "This is my beloved son, in whom I am well pleased." For a few brief seconds, it seemed almost as though time stood still. Then the man turned and walked back the way he had come, and when he reached the bank to climb back to dry land, John regained his voice and said, "Behold, the Lamb of God." The strangest thing was that there were tears streaming down John's face, yet he looked happy.

We had no idea what this could possibly mean. We heard John telling the people that this was the man they had been waiting for. Everyone's eyes followed this man as he climbed up the bank of the river. Quietly, he continued walking, seemingly again deep in thought, as he went up through the path on the opposite side. Soon he was out of sight. Our men discussed this for awhile, but no one seemed too interested. For some unfathomable reason, I could not keep my mind off what I had just witnessed. I strolled casually down to the riverbank and went to see John. I asked him who that man was he had just baptized. John looked at me suspiciously, as all the Jews did when facing a Roman soldier. Most Jewish men would either ignore me or defy me as much as he was legally able to do, but John simply looked at me very deeply. He seemed satisfied that I was genuinely interested, and not just idly curious. He told me, "That was Jesus of Nazareth, my cousin, but also much, much more." When I pressed him for more information, he simply told me to wait and eventually the entire world would know.

It finally struck me later as we prepared to camp for the night, this must have been the same Jesus that had been at Cana some weeks before, that had supposedly caused plain water to be changed into delicious wine. What manner of man could this be, if all this were true? What could be the meaning of the glowing light surrounding him, the voice from the sky, and all the signs that I had personally witnessed? From the depths of my being, I knew that I wanted to meet with this Jesus and ask him these questions personally.

We spent the next few days in that location, watching for signs of rebellion. When none seemed to be developing, our commander decided that we were not needed there any longer, and we began the march back to our headquarters.

Witnessing Healing Miracles

Word of Jesus spread very rapidly throughout the area. We sometimes happened to be patrolling some of the places where he was teaching, and I had many times heard him telling the people wonderful stories of a life without pain or worry, and it was all within our grasp. Most of the things he talked about were totally foreign to my beliefs, yet there was such a ring of truth in what he said, I couldn't help being interested in what he said, and wanting to learn more. He spoke as though there was only one God, instead of the numerous gods that we Romans revered. He also talked about this God as a loving father, who knows all our needs and wants to help us, if we only turn to him and follow his commandments.

My father had seen Jesus on several occasions, and listened to his teaching. He was most impressed with the seemingly impossible things that Jesus could do, though. He watched as Jesus went through crowds of people, most of whom were imploring him to heal them. Blind people suddenly could see, deaf people could hear, crippled people came to their feet and walked around, and even lepers claimed that he had cleansed them of their affliction. Father was so enthralled with these new philosophies and teachings, that he journeyed wherever Jesus was teaching, when he was close enough to where Father lived. Father brought home many stories of marvelous things that he had seen with his own eyes. Most of them seemed so impossible that I dismissed them as wishful thinking on his part. I continued to ponder all that he talked about, though.

Since our family home was in the city of Joppa, and Father traveled to various cities on his trade route, I was able to visit him fairly often. He had a small house in Capernaum, where he often stayed on his trips, and I visited frequently there. Most of the Roman soldiers were virtual exiles in this hostile land, but to me it was home. Whenever I had a week or two relief from my duties, I would spend this time with my family. One time I was granted an entire week off, and went to the home of my father in Capernaum. I was there about three days when I began to feel very ill. We were reclining at the table one evening, and I felt very dizzy and could hardly see. I tried to tell my father that I would like to be excused and go to my room to bed, but as I began to rise, I must have fainted, for I cannot remember anything after that time.

I was put to bed and Father sent for a physician. All this was told to me later, because I have no recollection whatever of all the things that transpired. The physician said that I had a very serious illness, something that most of the people living in that area seemed not to be affected by. I had become very feverish, and was beginning to rave. Sweat ran from every area of my body, and I sank very rapidly. The physician told my father very gravely that it appeared that I was not going to recover from this ailment.

Father issued orders then to the servants. One was dispatched to Jerusalem to tell Longinus that I was deathly ill and would probably not survive. Others were to tend me at the bedside, bathing me and trying to keep me comfortable while the physician stayed with me and monitored my rapidly deteriorating condition. Father also sent out several servants to find out if Jesus was teaching anywhere near the area. Over the next few hours, my breathing became labored, and I could not move my limbs. My father was told that I would probably be dead within a few more hours, and to prepare himself.

One servant returned and told Father that Jesus was teaching in Cana. It was within fast traveling distance, so Father immediately left us and went there. Arriving there, he followed the crowds of people that always poured out to see Jesus. Many people with various infirmities were painfully making their way to see and hear him. Father went right up to him in desperation and asked him if he could heal his son. Father told me that Jesus looked at him and he almost felt like he had been pierced by a sword, but the look was kindly. Jesus asked him if he wished him to come to his son, and my father replied, "Sir, come down before my child dies" Jesus then turned to the crowd and praised my father for his complete faith. He turned back to my father and told him, "You may go, your son will live." Father accepted his word without question and headed back home.

When Father approached the house, many of his servants rushed out happily to tell him that I had recovered. I can recall this time, when it seemed that I woke from a deep sleep, and looked around at all the attendants and wondered what they were all doing in my room. I can remember being extremely thirsty and asking for water. Next I felt that I needed some food. The servants brought many things to tempt my appetite, but I was so hungry that it needed no encouraging. The physician who was still there kept watching me with a very puzzled look on his face. He cautioned me against getting up, but I felt so strong that I could not stand to recline in bed any longer. Father came to me and embraced me with tears of joy on his face, which made me wonder, because I had no memory of being ill. He asked the servants exactly what hour it was when I had become healed. They told him, and he nodded sagely, saying, "That is right, that is the exact time that Jesus said he would be healed."

They told me how many days I had been ill, and how close to death I had been. Since I felt so well and strong, I could hardly believe it. I knew that my week of leave had passed, and I had to get back to my garrison. With the physician still clucking over me, I readied myself for the trip back to Jerusalem and wondered how I could explain all this to Longinus. When I arrived there, he took one look at me and scoffed, "Hah! Just as I suspected! You thought you would get a few extra days' leave by sending word that you were very ill. You certainly don't look like you have been sick at all, let alone near death!"

I told Longinus the same story that they had told me. How ill I was, how I sank very close to death, and how my father had desperately sought out Jesus to ask him to heal me. I explained to Longinus that this was the same man whom we had heard about before in Cana, when we enjoyed the delicious wine. That I had personally witnessed many other things that Jesus did. That many in my troop had also witnessed many impossible things. Finally, Longinus grudgingly accepted my explanations, saying that he, too, had seen and heard things that seemed impossible. Even though there must have been some trickery or magic of some kind, many people had seen and heard, and what they had not seen or heard themselves, they repeated what was told to them by others who had. Longinus curtly told me to get back to my duties, and he turned abruptly back to the orders that he had spread out on his table.

In carrying out my duties over the next few months, I continued to see Jesus from time to time. In order to get closer to him, on three occasions I disguised myself in peasant clothing and listened to what he taught. Each time I heard him speak, I felt the absolute rightness of his words. I realized that if everyone lived the way he told them was the right way, there would be no need of soldiers any longer. Everyone would care for each other, helping where help was needed, and it would be a totally different world than what we were used to. My heart swelled with longing for this type of life, and I caught myself wondering how I could begin to live like that myself.

Every time that Jesus taught, there was always a steady stream of ill and desperate people clamoring for him to heal them. I marveled at his patience and his seeming concern for each and every one of them. No matter how many hours it took, he never seemed to tire in his care for each person. One time there was a huge crowd listening to him speak, and I had been standing as close as I could to hear every word he spoke. I saw two of his disciples approach him and express concern for the crowd, and that they would be hungry. He spoke briefly to them and they appeared shocked. I heard one man say, "But there is no way we have enough money to feed this huge crowd."

Jesus motioned to a boy who had a basket beside him. The boy brought the basket to Jesus, who then told his disciples to have all the people recline and they were to distribute the food. The disciples eyed that small basket nervously, knowing that there couldn't be enough food in there to fill even five people. However, I watched Jesus as he confidently raised his eyes and prayed to his God. Then he gave the basket to the disciples, who took out a fish and handed it to someone. They took out another fish, and some bread, and as they continued to give the bread and fish to the people, the basket seemed almost to overflow. Eventually, every one of that huge crowd was eating happily until they were satisfied. Jesus told his disciples to gather up the remnants, so they wouldn't waste any food that could be given to the poor. I watched in amazement as they gathered up twelve baskets of what remained! How could this be? I saw exactly how much the boy had to begin with, and what was left was over ten times as much.

When I went back to my garrison, I was bursting with this miracle, but had no one that I could talk to. The only way that I could keep from exploding was to sit and write a letter to my Father, telling him all that I had seen that day. I knew that he would understand, since he had seen so many miraculous things as well. I could not get this out of my mind for many days.

Healing Longinus' Servant

Things had settled down and become fairly routine and quiet, as much as could be expected while trying to keep order among some of these rebellious people. One day I was working in the home of Longinus. As a centurion and leader of an entire century of soldiers, he was able to live in quarters away from the garrison at Jerusalem. Part of my duties as his aide was to handle much of his correspondence. I was busily writing to one of his friends in Rome when Longinus entered the room, seeming very agitated.

"Remember my servant Marcellus, whom I have raised since he was a child?" he asked me. "Of course," I replied, "All of us in the century know him. He seems almost to be your son, instead of your servant." Longinus agreed with me that this was the case. He said that now Marcellus himself seemed to have fallen victim to the same sort of malady that I had overcome. His physician had told him that there was hardly any chance that Marcellus would recover, and that Longinus should prepare himself for his death.

Longinus asked me for more details about the healing that I had experienced. I recounted all that I could remember, but also told him what my father had related to me, about his visit to Jesus of Nazareth. How this Jesus had been astounded at the faith that my father had in his powers, and how he then promised my father that his faith had been rewarded. I had been healed, and the servants said that it was at the exact time that my father had been speaking to Jesus. Longinus pressed me for every last shred of the story, and seemed to be bracing himself for some action.

"Come with me," he said. "I will also go to see this miracle man, and ask him if he can heal my servant in the same way that he cured you." With very little preparation, just the two of us, with only two guards as protection, made our way to the area where we had heard that Jesus was staying at this time. Just outside the town, we saw a crowd of people as usual, surrounding a man and listening to what he was saying. Many crippled and deformed people were painfully making their way to him as well, in hopes that their ailments and afflictions would be lifted from them.

As we made our way to Jesus, the crowd parted around us, since we were the hated oppressors of these people. Jesus looked up to see us, and he gazed straight into my eyes. He seemed to see something that he recognized, as he smiled at me. I felt a strange tingling in my body and could not seem to break the gaze. Jesus then turned his eyes on Longinus. He seemed suddenly to be sad, but he greeted Longinus warmly, again with a smile that seemed truly sincere. He exhibited none of the animosity toward us that the bulk of the population had.

Longinus, in his usual straightforward and blunt manner, walked up to Jesus and told him about his servant. He asked Jesus if it would be possible for him to cure Marcellus. Jesus looked at him steadily and then replied, "Of course; I will come to your house with you." Then Longinus amazed me with his response, "Lord, I am not worthy that you should come under my roof. If you but say the word, I know that my servant will be healed." Jesus then turned and spoke to the crowd, marveling at the faith that was shown by a Roman and a heathen. He then turned back to Longinus and they spoke softly for a few minutes. Then I heard Jesus say, "Go to your home. Your servant is healed."

With deep gratitude and faith that this was true, Longinus thanked Jesus and we turned to go back to his house. We talked about the power that we both felt coming from this strange man, and discussed some of the things we had heard him talking about. Unlike most of the rabble rousers, Jesus was preaching peace and love for one another. He told the people that they should care for each other, and help anyone that needed it. He spoke as though every man on earth was of great value to God. This was very strange to us as Romans, because we knew that there were many gods that controlled our lives. The idea of having one God only, and that one being like a loving father to us, was totally foreign.

There was a sense of serenity about Longinus that I had never observed before. As we drew closer to his home, we saw three of his other servants rushing to us, babbling excitedly. They said, "He is healed. Marcellus is cured. He is up and around and acts like there was never anything wrong with him." Longinus looked at me and smiled, and said, "I was certain that Jesus had the power to do this, even though I don't know how." We went into the house and Longinus greeted Marcellus lovingly. Marcellus was like I had been when I was healed, having no idea of how seriously ill he had been. He knew he was not feeling well, and then felt that he had just been sleeping and woke up totally well again.

Longinus and I both pondered these events for a long time. We could only talk to each other about these things, because we were the only Romans that so far had been touched in such an intimate way by this man, Jesus. Any of the soldiers would have laughed and ridiculed us behind our backs. We had to be very careful, but we could not deny what we had seen and experienced. I was relieved that at least now I had someone that I could talk to and relate some other things that I had witnessed. The more we discussed Jesus, the more mixed feelings I began to have. I found myself wondering about the possibility of there being only one God. Jesus seemed to be so sure of this, and so confident in his teaching, that it began to seem more and more that it could be true.

The Arrest of Jesus

The Roman garrison within the fortress of Antonia at Jerusalem had been strengthened to the limit for the Jewish Passover celebration. For a week before this ritual, people began streaming into the city, staying with friends or relatives, or setting up temporary shelters outside the city walls. It seemed that the entire population of all Palestine was in Jerusalem, and tensions were high. Many people were openly hostile and aggressive toward the soldiers. Our leaders worked with the Jewish religious leaders who enlisted their own temple guards to help us control the people. With the temple guards stationed on the temple grounds, we could send fewer men there, and reinforce other areas of the city where there was much unrest. At times like this, it seemed as though the city itself was like a boiling pot. It seethed and simmered, and always threatened to break out into a full, rolling boil that would erupt and scald indiscriminately.

Longinus ordered his century of soldiers to guard the various gates leading into the city. At any moment when things became too dangerous, a runner could be dispatched to the nearest group for reinforcements. We had gone over our orders very carefully, and all the soldier's nerves were stretched very thin. Some of the soldiers took out their frustrations on the people, whether they were doing anything wrong or not. We had to watch for this too, because it wouldn't take much provocation to cause a full scale riot.

We were on the walls above the city, patrolling from above and watching for any suspicious moves. Suddenly we heard singing and cheering, and a great disturbance. Thinking this might be the rebellion we all worried about, we quickly looked to see what was the cause of this noise. There was a tremendous crowd of people throwing their cloaks on the ground and waving palms around as they sang. In their midst, we saw a man sitting on a donkey, riding into the city. I heard many of the people shouting, "Hail to the King!" "Hosanna to the son of David!" "Make way for the salvation of Israel." We were certain that this meant trouble, yet none of the people seemed angry or had anything that could be used as weapons.

As the donkey approached the gate under the wall where I stood, I saw that the rider on its back was Jesus. He rode quietly, with his head down, and almost seemed sorrowful. With all the joyous shouting and singing around him, I couldn't understand it. He did lift his hand in blessing of the people as he passed, and countless hands reached out to touch him as he rode by. The same group of men that always surrounded him was following him closely. I recognized them as his apostles, as they were called by the people. Most of them seemed far happier than Jesus did, and one of them that we knew as Judas of Kerioth actually leaped in the air with elation. As we realized that this crowd was peaceful and did not pose any threat, we relaxed somewhat.

Longinus rode up to us on his favorite horse, pushing his way through the crowd. He told us that any man that could command such a large crowd was dangerous, and that we needed to watch him carefully. His orders came from the Governor himself, who had been in several deep discussions with the local religious leaders. I knew that Longinus shared the same feelings that I had concerning Jesus, but orders had to be obeyed. Consequently, we dispatched a group of soldiers to follow the crowd and keep a careful eye on Jesus.

Insurrections and hostile actions seemed to spring up all over the city. We no sooner had one disturbance quelled, than we were called to another area to put down another riot. These people were absolutely unbelievable in their radical beliefs and in the open rebellion they were showing more and more confidently.

One day we were stationed close to the temple along with the Jewish temple guards. Even though they were hostile to us, they welcomed our presence there, knowing that we could keep the peace with force if necessary. I stood on the wall overlooking the temple and heard a roar of protest. I could hear wood crashing and voices shouting, and checked to see what was happening. Amazingly, I saw this peaceful man, Jesus, pushing over tables, spilling money, freeing animals, and whipping the men who sat in the temple changing money and selling animals for sacrifice. This was totally out of character for him, who was always preaching peace and love and selfless behavior. The temple guards seemed to be outraged, while my soldiers and I all grinned with enjoyment. We moved in to prevent a serious riot, but by the time we got there, Jesus had disappeared and had left a shambles behind. He had certainly put a stop to any more of the money gouging that we knew was going on in the temple court. Secretly, I admired Jesus for having the courage to rise against that group, which was growing rich on the needs of the people. I couldn't help feeling sympathetic to his thoughts, whatever they were.

As the days went on, tensions mounted accordingly. Many of us were serving two shifts a day to help keep order. We were all looking forward to their Passover, which was supposed to happen in the next two days. After that celebration, most of the visitors would be leaving the city, and it would once again settle back to a more normal state, with uprisings occurring only once a week or so, instead of several times each day. All of us were tired and looking forward to the end of this week.

That evening, Longinus was visited by a group of Jewish religious leaders. They presented a paper giving us authority to arrest Jesus and bring him to the Sanhedrin for trial. We could not believe it, because we could see nothing that Jesus had done to deserve arrest. Perhaps he went too far in cleaning out the temple of the dishonest money changers. Whatever the reason, we had our orders. The only difficulty was how to find one man in this crowded city. When Longinus mentioned this to them, they brought one of Jesus' own disciples to us. I saw that it was Judas of Kerioth, and he had promised to lead the soldiers to the place where he knew that Jesus would be.

We gathered our unit of troops to follow Judas. Many of the temple guards and some of the priests insisted on coming along as well. Since it was dark and the hour was getting late, we had some of the men carrying torches. We marched through the city, shouldering many people out of the way as we went. We went through the Golden Gate and into the Kidron Valley, and from there east toward the Mount of Olives. There was a Garden there named Gethsemane, where Judas assured us that we would find Jesus. After passing through the numerous tents that had been set up outside the city walls, the night became very quiet and peaceful. It was cool after a very hot day, and the slight breeze was refreshing. In the distance, I could hear a jackal howl, and far off barking of dogs challenging it. Night creatures all made their variety of muted sounds, and the air was perfumed with the scent of flowers mixed with an underlying smell of honey. It was a wonderfully peaceful and enjoyable walk after the stress of dealing with the yowling crowds all week. Yet, I found myself full of apprehension at the necessity of arresting the man Jesus. After all, I was especially favored by him at my healing. I knew Longinus was thinking these same thoughts as well, wondering at the vagaries of the system we worked under.

As we entered the Garden, we noticed several men beneath the trees wrapped in their cloaks, sleeping. When they heard the noise we were making, they sprang up and began shouting. Three more men came from behind them, and beyond them we could see Jesus, walking toward us. Judas broke away from our formation and ran toward Jesus, kissing him on the cheek. Jesus looked at him and said, "Do you betray the son of man with a kiss, Judas?" and he seemed to be suffering from some deep emotional pain. Jesus turned to us and said, "Who are you looking for?" One of the priests replied, "Jesus of Nazareth." "I am he," Jesus stated, and unaccountably, every one of us was knocked off our feet onto the ground. I thought at first that I had been clumsy and stumbled, and I was embarrassed to be seen on the ground. As I looked around, though, I saw everyone else on the ground too, looking at each other in embarrassment and amazement. None of us could imagine the force we had just been exposed to, and the closest thing to it that I can describe is as if a giant hand had simply pushed us down. As we scrambled back to our feet, Jesus again spoke, "You are looking for Jesus of Nazareth. I have told you that I am he. Let these other men go."

Suddenly one of Jesus' disciples rushed toward us with his sword drawn. One of the servants was standing there with a torch raised high to help us see. The sword slashed, the servant ducked, but blood spurted out from his head, and we could see that his ear had been severed and was lying on the ground. "No, Peter!" admonished Jesus. "Put away your sword. Those that live by the sword shall die by the sword." Jesus then picked up the severed ear, bent over the sobbing servant, and placed one hand on his shoulder, while with the other, he replaced the ear. A startled look came over the servant's face, and he stopped sobbing. Jesus stood up and once again told us to take him. We were so stunned by what he had done that it took awhile to recover enough to put him in bonds. The servant's ear was back in place, the blood was gone, and there wasn't a sign that it had been cut off. We all feared power such as this, and yet, Jesus wasn't offering any resistance to us at all.

The priests told us to take Jesus to the house of Ananias, where several had been gathered to hear charges against him. As soon as we arrived there, Longinus and I and our troop were relieved by another group of soldiers. Our shift was over and we were to return to the Fort of Antonia to fortify ourselves with rest, because we knew that we would be on duty all day on the following day.

Jesus' Suffering and Death

The next morning when we went on duty, we were told to report immediately to the prison section of the fort. It seemed that during the night, the Jews had been marching from one end of the city to another with Jesus, taking him to Pontius Pilate, then to King Herod, back to the Jewish priests, and on and on. No one could seem to find just cause for his arrest, yet the priests continued to clamor for his death. Longinus and I could only talk about our feelings to each other, because the other soldiers would have thought we were totally crazy. The situation at this time was that Governor Pilate had in desperation ordered Jesus to be scourged, in order to appease the crowd.

As Longinus and I arrived at the prison with our freshly-rested soldiers, we could see Jesus tied to one of the pillars supporting the roof. He hung from his bound arms and it was obvious that he had lapsed into unconsciousness. And no wonder, since it appeared that the men assigned to the scourging had taken out most of their aggression on this one man who happened to be in their power. I could see that they had used the flagella, a whip with several leather thongs attached to the handle. Each leather thong had something attached to the tip. The things that were used were bits of stone, leather knots, sharp objects like broken sword pieces, and other things that could be used to cut, bruise, or otherwise cause excruciating pain. Jesus' back looked like raw meat, and there was a lot of blood on the floor around him.

Longinus asked what the situation was, and the officer in charge reported to him. "We were ordered to give this man 39 lashes, and every time he passed out, we let him rest for awhile, and then splashed cold water on him so that he could enjoy the punishment as much as we all did." Longinus questioned, "Has he had his 39 lashes? It looks almost like you have doubled it." The officer answered, "Well we are sure we gave him 39, but I think we kind of lost count after that." Longinus then ordered his men to take Jesus away from the pillar. We were told that we had to take him back to Governor Pilate so that he could present him to the people with proof that he had been severely punished. One soldier revived Jesus with another splash of cold water, and they led him to a bench where he could sit down. I could see he was very weak, and his legs trembled as he tried to make his way without assistance.

The men were all beginning to torment Jesus and called him their king in a very mocking way. One of them grabbed a cloak and put it around Jesus' shoulders. Jesus stared straight ahead but seemed grateful for the warmth of the cloak. He was shivering and exhibiting many of the symptoms that I had seen in men wounded in battle that were close to death. As the men danced around him bowing and mocking, he looked off into the distance and moved his lips again. One ingenious fellow decided that a king needed a crown, and proceeded to bend twigs from a thorn bush into a circlet. He brought this circlet over to Jesus and placed it on his head. Then he used a rod to push it down securely. The thorns sank deep into the flesh of Jesus' head, and he gasped with the pain, as fresh blood began to trickle down each thorn puncture and made small rivulets of blood on his face.

After Jesus had rested and regained some strength, we took him back to show him to Pontius Pilate. Pilate looked at him and spoke to him in our tongue, and seemed surprised when Jesus answered in the same tongue. The crowd was thronging through the courtyard, yelling and shaking their fists. It seemed that everyone there hated Jesus, and only a small voice could be heard here and there in support of him. These voices were quickly stifled.

Pilate then took Jesus and showed him to the crowd. He thought they would be appeased at the sight of the bloody, tortured man. Instead, they seemed to redouble their frenzied calls for his death. In desperation, Pilate ordered one of the worst criminals in the prison to be brought forth. He called upon a Jewish custom of releasing one prisoner to them at the time of Passover. When the guards brought Bar Abbas to stand next to him, I felt that Jesus was certainly safe. After all, this Bar Abbas was a hardened criminal, guilty of robbery, murder, and who knew what else.

Pilate asked who should be released, and the crowd, as though it had been rehearsed, screamed, "Bar Abbas! Bar Abbas!" Perplexed, Pilate asked them, "What, then, should I do with this Jesus?" All they could do was shout, "Crucify him! Crucify him!" Pilate had found no reason to even have Jesus imprisoned, and he was bewildered about the crowd's reactions. He was politically shrewd enough to realize that he had to keep the people somewhat appeased in order to better keep the peace.

Pilate considered his own position and made his decision. He simply could not afford to have serious rebellion problems on his hands. That would definitely put a halt to his career. He called for one of his servants to bring him a bowl of water. He put his hands in the water and said, "I do not wish to have the blood of an innocent man on my hands." A band of men at the center of the crowd screamed, "Let his blood be upon us and upon our people!" Pilate then said, "So be it," and gave the orders for another crucifixion.

The events that followed that day have been etched into my memory so that I can recall every second, every action, every shout, and every emotion that I experienced then. I don't know how many times that I have re-lived that day over and over, and each time with such a sense of wonder, pain, and other emotions, some that I could not name.

Two other criminals had been crucified previously, and they were still hanging on their crosses at the top of the hill called Golgotha. Another cross was brought out and laid on Jesus' shoulders, so that he could carry his own up to the top of the hill. As we started down the narrow streets, people were lined up all along the way. There was constant shouting and weeping, as well as curses as we walked along. Some of the Jewish priests rode along on their donkeys to witness the death of Jesus. Once, one of the women in the crowd broke through our ranks and gently wiped Jesus' face with a cloth dampened in cool water. He smiled at her gratefully and gave her a blessing. I was amazed at the way he was concerned with the people along the way, and seemed not to even consider his own suffering.

Jesus had lost a lot of blood during the scourging, and was very weak. Twice he fell under the cross, and when one of the soldiers began whipping him to make him get up, Longinus stopped him. "Can you not see that this man is almost at the point of death?" Jesus struggled to his feet each time, but the third time he fell, he simply lay there as though he was already dead. Longinus looked at the crowd, and singled out a burly man who looked very strong. "You there!" he said, "Help this man carry the cross to the top of the hill." The man began to protest, but then Jesus looked at him. For a few seconds, they just stared into each other's eyes. Then the man took the cross and Jesus smiled at him as they continued on the way to the top of the hill. All during the winding path, I was wrestling with my own thoughts. Why was this man condemned to death? Had he ever done anything but good to people? Why did the crowd seem so bent on putting him to death? Especially after the way they had welcomed him to Jerusalem just a few days before this. Not for the first time, I began to resent my status as a soldier. My own mind and heart were telling me that Jesus was a good man. He should not be struggling along to his own death. And I was one of the Roman soldiers carrying out his death sentence. I was torn in many directions as we traveled upward.

At one point, I felt that my heart would be torn from my body. This was when the mother of Jesus met him on the road to his death. She spoke to him gently and tenderly and seemed to be trying to take on some of his pain. Jesus was so exhausted that he could scarcely speak at this time, but he murmured some words to her. The soldiers told her to get out of the way, and she stood to one side with tears streaming down her face. I felt like the most wretched person on earth for the orders I was following.

Finally, we reached the hill where the other two criminals were hanging on their crosses. There was an area between these two that was open, where we could place another. Two of our soldiers pulled off all of Jesus' clothes, and they threw him on the ground on top of his cross, so that he could be nailed to it. I was thankful that I did not have to have anything to do physically to assist in Jesus' death. I was directly under Longinus, and it was up to us to see that orders were carried out. The soldiers were coarse men, bored with their assignment in this horrid country, and seemed to take pleasure in what they did. I did not think that I could carry out the orders if I were told to take up the nails and do the actual crucifixion.

The soldiers began to stretch out Jesus' hands and carefully placed nails through his wrists, being sure that they didn't go through a bone or anywhere that might cause too much bleeding. All during this nailing process, not a sound came from Jesus. He would gasp and inhale sharply, but not cry out. They put his feet on a raised part of the cross so he could support his weight on them. Then they nailed his feet to that part. After all this was done, they raised the cross and set it in place. I knew that each movement would be causing extreme agony, yet he never cried out. Instead, as soon as the cross was fixed firmly in the ground, Jesus looked to the sky and said, "Father, forgive them, for they do not know what they are doing."

Generally, after the crucifixion, we were free to go back to other duties. Because of the priest's demands, or whatever reason, we were ordered to stay there until the criminals were dead. They said it had something to do with their holy day, and no man should be allowed to hang on the cross after this particular evening. These people with their hundreds of rules were always a source of amusement to the troops. Most of the soldiers passed the time playing dice. This was the most boring part of a crucifixion, waiting for the sentenced one to die. Longinus and I stood apart talking about the events, and we were both in agreement that something was seriously wrong with the way Jesus was being treated. But, being soldiers and used to obeying orders, we could do nothing about it.

Crucifixion was a very slow, torturous way to die. It generally took several days, and the cause of death was either from dehydration, exposure, or suffocation. The man would hang from his arms, causing his head to drop to his chest. The lungs could not get enough air, and when the body began to demand to take a breath of air, the man had to raise himself up using his feet, lift his body and head in order to take a breath. When a man became too weak to raise himself up, he literally suffocated. If he was strong enough to last several days, he could die from lack of food, but especially water. In this place, especially in the summer, the heat would kill more rapidly when the person was deprived of water. At night, it could also become very cold, and the changes in temperature, combined with lack of food, clothing, or water, could be deadly.

Some women had been following us all the way and watched while Jesus was being nailed and raised on the cross. They were weeping and wailing, and we noticed that one of them was the mother of Jesus. She was a small, slender woman, with the most beautiful eyes that I had ever seen. Her hair was dark with some streaks of grey but no other indication of her age. Even though she was weeping and under great stress, she seemed to be working hard to maintain control. Next to her were two other women who were also weeping. They all clung to one another for comfort and support. Beside the women was a youth, whom I took to be perhaps eight years younger than myself. Jesus actually spoke to them at least twice during those hours.

At one point in the afternoon, Jesus cried out that he was thirsty. I knew that he had not been given water during his captivity and beating, and with the loss of blood, he must have been in terrible agony. Thinking quickly, I attached a sponge to the tip of my spear, and soaked it in water. I then sprinkled an herb on it which was a local opiate, and I knew it would ease his pain at least a little. As I raised it to his lips, he looked at me, and I felt that he could see me inside and out, and even know what I was thinking. He touched his lips to the sponge, but he could taste the opiate in it, and he spat it out. He looked at me again as if to tell me that he actually WANTED to feel every nuance of pain that was coursing through his body. I felt such emotional torment, and looking at him, had the strange sensation that he was comforting me.

The other men on their crosses began talking to Jesus. One of them was ridiculing him and cursing him, telling him that if he really was the Messiah, why couldn't he save himself and them, too. The other one rebuked him, and said, "After all, you and I have committed crimes, and we deserve this punishment, but this man has done nothing wrong, and should not even be here." Then he turned to Jesus and said, "Rabbi, remember me when you come into your kingdom." Jesus painfully pushed himself up to breathe and speak, and said, "I say to you, this day you shall see me in paradise." And then he lapsed into silence once more. I had even more things to ponder over and try to find answers for. What was this place he continued to speak about, where one would go when he died?

Jesus then seemed to be concerned for his mother. With his death, who would support her? A woman without a man in her house, unless she happened to be wealthy, would certainly die. He called out to his mother and pointed out the young man standing with her. He said, "Woman, behold your son." Then he looked at the young man, and said, "Behold your mother." The young man blinked back tears but moved to put his arm around Jesus' mother, to show that he would follow the orders given to him.

During the hours we were there, the weather grew more and more strange. There was a strange, unearthly glow cast upon the earth from the unusual cloud formations above us. The air became very still, and the heat was oppressive. Sounds of those close by began to seem muffled, while those from far away became sharper. At some times, I felt the hairs on my body raise again, and it seemed as though when I looked at Jesus, that I was looking down a long tunnel at him and he was very far away. Then I blinked my eyes, and he was back right in front of me again.

As the afternoon began to wear on, Longinus told me that we would have to break the legs of all the men, so that they would die at once and could be taken off the crosses for the Jewish holy day celebration. About that time, Jesus raised his head and said, "It is finished," his head dropped, and we couldn't see him moving again. Longinus said it was amazing that he lived that long, because of all the blood that he had already lost. He ordered his men to break the other two criminal's legs, and we could hear the sickening sounds of bone breaking, to the accompaniment of screaming from the tortured men.

When the soldier came to Jesus to break his legs, Longinus ordered them away. "He is already dead," he explained. Then he took his lance and told me that he would make sure that Jesus was dead. I protested, "How can you cause more pain to this innocent man who has already suffered so much?" Longinus said, "First of all, I am certain that he lives no longer. Next, this lance prick will hurt far less than having his legs broken, I can assure you." I saw the logic in that, and stood next to Longinus as he thrust his lance deep into Jesus side, through the lungs and directly into the heart.

Water mixed with blood came out of the wound, and splashed all over both of us. I cannot explain how that felt. It was warm, and comforting, and soothing, and energizing all at the same time. I wanted to stand there forever, bathed in that wonderful liquid. Longinus and I looked at each other, and I am sure that he had felt the same things that I had, judging from the look on his face. I felt as though I were being washed clean from every piece of dust and grime that had entered my life.

Before we could discuss anything further, the sky turned black as night. Lightning flashed all over the sky, and thunder rolled and boomed. The ground began to shake under our feet. People started screaming in fear and running about, trying to find safe shelter. The priests who had been there observing the death muttered among themselves and began chanting prayers. You could see that they too, were terrified. Only the women and the young man who had been talking to Jesus seemed unafraid. Grief-stricken, yes, but they actually looked as though they expected these things. The ground split in places, and tombs were broken open. After a few minutes of absolute terror, the sky cleared again, and all appeared serene once more. Cornelius, one of the soldiers that had been involved in the crucifixion, actually was heard to say, "Truly, this man must have been the son of God."

One of the wealthier men in Jerusalem appeared on the scene. His name was Joseph, from Arimathea, and he was often seen in the crowds listening to Jesus. He strode over to the family standing by Jesus' cross, and spoke to them. He then came to us, and told us that he had offered his tomb for the family in which to place the body of Jesus. He showed us the official order, signed by the High Priest and the Governor, so we were able to release the body to him. Several other people had gathered by this time, and were helping the soldiers taking down all three bodies. It mattered not to me where they took the others, but I was ordered to stay with Jesus and see to it that he was properly placed in a sealed tomb.

The family wrapped Jesus' body in a large burial shroud, and began to carry him to the cave where Joseph's tomb was. It wasn't too far away from the hill of Golgotha; we walked down past a garden area, around some winding paths, and finally ended up in a cul de sac, at the end of which was the cave. The cave had been dug out of the hillside, and the cliff above it reached straight up. We could see there was no way that anyone could get near the place from above. Anyone would have to follow the same winding path that we had. As they placed the body inside the tomb, further orders were brought to us. We were now ordered to keep watch over the tomb.

Longinus was thoroughly disgusted by this time. He cursed, "They have already killed this righteous man, why do they now need us to guard his dead body?" The owner of the tomb explained that the priests had persuaded Herod and Pilate both to have the tomb guarded, because the priests were afraid that Jesus' followers would steal in during the night and remove his body, claiming that he had raised himself from the dead. Our orders were to stand guard there for the next 10 days, by which time the putrefaction would be so bad, that no one would be brave enough to raid the tomb. Consequently, we were given shifts of 12 hours each to stand guard over a dangerous dead man!

The next two days dragged on tediously. At least things were quiet during the Jewish holy day celebration. Hardly anyone could be seen on the streets, so it didn't matter that several soldiers were taken away from the city walls to stand guard over a tomb. After they had laid the body of Jesus inside the cave, four strong men struggled with a huge stone, rolling it in front of the cave entrance, so there was no possibility of anyone being able to sneak in and open the cave. If four of our strongest men were needed to push it in place, it should take at least a half dozen others to move it out of the way again. A squad of ten soldiers was assigned to each half-day shift, and everyone passed the time in various ways.

The Resurrection

As it turned out, the squadron that I commanded was on duty on the third night after Jesus' death. It would have been impossible for every one of us to remain awake for the entire 12 hour shift, so I assigned three groups of three men each to take turns staying on duty at night. That way, many of the soldiers could get some rest during the shift, and still be able to remain alert and watchful during this most boring assignment.

About an hour or so before dawn of the third day, I was on guard with the three men that were assigned to that segment of duty. We had built a small fire for warmth, and were sitting in front of it and talking, making sure that we were all awake. We talked about some of the campaigns that we had been on, many of the battles we had seen, anything to keep us awake and alert. I got up about this time to go into the bushes to relieve myself, so I was away from the campfire, and it cannot be blamed for what happened next.

As I completed my task and turned away from the bushes, I took two steps and then looked up at the sky, to see if I could see any trace of the approaching day. It was still pitch dark, with not even a trace of a moon. There were clouds covering the sky so not even a star shed any light. I did see one light above me, and I looked with curiosity to see what it might be. The light began to get closer, and suddenly my hairs all stood up again. I felt the ground tremble slightly beneath my feet. It wasn't like an earthquake this time. It was more like the tingling sensation you feel when you see something approaching that you have been anticipating for a long time. The light then split into two lights, and they continued to move closer.

I became aware that all night noises had suddenly ceased. Not a sound could be heard anywhere. I looked at my men and saw that the ones on guard duty had also noticed the unusual things that I had been aware of, and were watching the lights as intently as I. The rest of the men were soundly sleeping, but even they had ceased their snoring. It was as though perhaps our ears were completely stopped up, since not a single sound penetrated. Once again, the hairs on my body seemed to raise and quiver, as I stood spellbound.

The lights moved closer, and the hairs on my body continued tingling. I began to see shapes inside the lights. In fact, the light seemed to come from inside whatever the shape was. Then I saw two very large beings shimmering inside the lights, and they floated to the rock covering the tomb, one on each side. I could not move a muscle, and it seemed that I had actually even stopped breathing, but at the corner of my eye, saw that the other guards were affected the same way that I was. We seemed to be turned to stone, and I am not sure that we were even breathing.

As the two beings touched the stone, it began to roll back away from the opening of the tomb. Then I saw light coming from INSIDE the cave, and I was struck with fear and terror. The two huge beings knelt on the ground, one on each side of the cave, and slowly, someone began to emerge from the cave. I knew this was totally impossible, and I wanted to run away, but my legs would not move. I could see Jesus, glowing with an interior light, coming out of his grave! I wanted to cry out, to fall on my knees, do anything to prove that I was alive, but not a muscle in my body would respond. Never had I been so paralyzed with fear.

As Jesus came fully into view, there was no mistaking him with the light all around him. He raised his hands in blessing to the two beings, and they bowed once again, then rose and ascended into the sky again. Jesus walked right by all the guards, and smiled gently at me as he saw me watching. He continued back on the winding path through the trees, and then was gone from view. The cave was now dark, with a darker space where the entrance was, which was now uncovered by the stone.

Finally, all those of us who were awake could move again. The men began chattering almost hysterically, and all of us kept telling each other that we had seen the same thing, and that none were insane. With the excited talking becoming increasingly louder, soon the entire squadron was awake. At last we could see tinges of light coming from the east, signaling the sun was about to rise. The soldiers looked at the tomb, and saw that the stone had been moved. They were just as fearful as the rest of us were, only they were afraid of what our commander would do when he learned that the tomb we were set to guard had indeed been broken into. They hurled curses and accusations at us, as though we were responsible for the tomb being opened.

Those of us who had been awake continued to tell our story, exactly the way we had all experienced it. The sleepers scoffed at us and refused to believe us, but we all knew that we had to make a report as soon as possible. As soon as it became light enough to see our way through the winding, rocky path, we gathered up our gear and started back to the fortress of Antonia, where Longinus was quartered. The three men who had been standing guard came with me to Longinus' room to tell him what we had seen. He sent a messenger to the Governor and to the High Priest before he questioned us more thoroughly. He kept looking very skeptical, but I know that he put more faith in my statements than that of the other men. After listening to all the reports from every one of us in turn, he took me aside and asked me to give him every last detail of what I had seen.

By the time I had finished with my story, several of the priests came rushing in, demanding to know what had happened to Jesus' body. The messenger had only told them that the tomb had been opened, and he didn't know any further details. Longinus looked at them and growled, "Well, it looks like one of your ancient prophecies has indeed come to pass. According to all the men who were present, not a single person came near the tomb, yet Jesus himself walked out after the stone had been rolled away." The priests muttered amongst themselves and demanded that we tell them the truth. When none of us would change our story, they huddled together and discussed the issue for awhile, then came back to our group.

"Take this money," offered the High Priest. "Make a solemn oath that you will tell no one of this night. If you are asked, simply say that you fell asleep and some of Jesus' followers must have slipped past you and stolen his body." The squadron all refused to do this. They knew that if they admitted that they had been asleep, they would all have been subjected to severe discipline. The High Priest then conceded, "Do not worry, we will make sure that you do not get into trouble over this. We have friends in enough places to ensure your safety in this matter." With this assurance, the soldiers all took the money offered to them. It was much wealth to them, amounting to almost a year's pay. Every one swore to say what the priests directed them to say, and when they were satisfied, the Jews all left.

Longinus dismissed the soldiers with the same admonition not to tell this ridiculous sounding story to anyone, and kept me in his room. After everyone left, he became much more animated, and wanted to talk more about the events of these past few days. He told me that he had been thinking long and deeply about all these things, and said, "You know, there has been nothing but strange happenings ever since I was stationed in this country. Remember that you yourself claim that you were near death, yet were completely healed simply at the word of this Jesus. My own servant recovered miraculously after I had gone to Jesus and asked him for help. I have seen men who were crippled get up and walk. I have seen blind men open their eyes and shout for joy at being able to see. The mute speak, the deaf hear, and I have even witnessed lepers being totally cleansed and healed in just a matter of seconds, at Jesus touch. I cannot explain to you what I felt when I thrust the spear into his side to make sure he was dead, and his blood and water sprayed over me. I vowed never again to use that spear, and I threw it on the ground in disgust.

"I guess what I am trying to say is that I have come to believe in the things that Jesus taught. I feel that his preaching about loving one another is the only right way to live, and with these thoughts, I don't see how I can continue to be a good soldier. In fact, I am asking for a transfer out of this country, because if I stay and keep feeling this way, my entire career will be in shambles."

I grasped Longinus' hands and told him that I had felt the same way. I believed even more than he did, and I could not even bear to be a soldier anywhere. I told him that I was planning on defecting from the army, and would try to find Jesus' followers to see if I could join them. He was very sympathetic, and told me that he would help as much as he could. He brought out some simple robes that the local people wore and told me that when I left his room I should remove my officer's garb and clothe myself in this peasant outfit. Since, as most Romans, I was clean-shaven, I would have to keep my head covering on and bow my head in shadows. He told me that as soon as I left, he would have to act as though I were dead, and he could not help me any further, or he would also be in serious trouble.

I left Longinus and took the bundle of clothes with me. I wandered back through the wild area where the tomb had been, thinking that I would need to get far away from everyone before I changed clothes. I would simply have to disappear, and I was trying to formulate plans as I walked along.

Meeting With Peter

As I approached the place near the tomb where we had camped the previous night, I heard excited voices. I drew back behind a tree to see who was there. Around the bushes ahead of me I saw the young man who had been standing at the cross with Jesus' mother. With him was an older man, and they were talking very rapidly in Aramaic. I had to strain to catch enough of their conversation so I knew what they were talking about. They said things about an empty tomb, wondering who could have done it and what they had done.

Before I knew what I was going to do, I felt compelled to step in front of them and announce my presence. As the two Jews saw a Roman soldier standing there, they stopped immediately and seemed to shrink away from me. I recognized the older man as Petrus, and I addressed him that way. Some force took over me in the same way that it had the night before, and I fell on my knees before him. I took his hands in mine and begged him to listen to me. He peered deeply into my eyes and then said, "Get up and come with us. We would all hear what you have to say."

The sight of a Roman soldier walking with Jews would not be uncommon in this city. I would just have to make it look like I was ordering them somewhere, and no one would challenge us, as long as I could avoid other soldiers who knew me. I didn't think anyone yet knew of my decision to defect except Longinus, and I knew that I could trust him.

We trudged into a poor section of the town, and Petrus, whom the followers all called Peter, went to a locked door and spoke to someone inside. There was some argument about opening the door, but Peter finally assured the guards that I was not a threat, and we must be let in before we drew a curious crowd. Finally, the door opened, and we went inside. We were in a small room with no light, and it took a few moments to become accustomed to the dimness. I could see steps leading up to an upper floor on my right, and straight ahead, a hall leading to what looked like normal family quarters.

Peter motioned me to follow him, and he started up the stairs. The young man that I had seen at the cross brought up the rear, followed by the man who had been guarding the door. At the top of the stairs there was a landing, and another closed door. Again Peter knocked and talked to someone inside. At last, we were all allowed into one large room, and there were around 20 men and women there. Some were sitting and talking, some were busy cooking, but all were staring at us as we entered the room. Some began to shrink back in fear at the sight of me, but Peter again hastened to reassure them.

When calm had been established, Peter told everyone that I had an eye witness report to make to all of them. He began by telling everyone, "Mary was right. John and I went to the tomb, and the stone had been rolled away, and Jesus was not there. We started back to town and met this soldier. He insisted that he had been guarding the tomb with several other men, and he actually saw Jesus walking out of the tomb by himself. He wants to tell all of us exactly what he saw, and what happened."

Thus, I began to relate my story. I started with my orders to be at the crucifixion, and later to stand guard over Jesus' tomb. I explained everything that I had seen and tried to explain some of the feelings that I had also experienced. I finished by telling them that I could no longer serve in the Roman army, and had defected. I threw myself on their mercy and asked if they could hide me for awhile. Peter looked at the clothing that Longinus had given me, and declared that it would be suitable. He told me that if I wanted to really blend in as a Jewish citizen, I would need to grow a beard and let my hair grow. This I readily agreed to.

So began my stay with Jesus' main group of followers. I met them all, and some of them accepted me, while others kept their distance. One of them, Thomas, openly disagreed with Peter for allowing me to stay there. All during that day, I had to repeat my story again and again, to all the people in the room. Some of them stayed to listen to the story more than once.

Once during the day, another lady that I had seen at the cross came into the room. They introduced her to me as Mary from Magdala. She had been raised in a very wealthy family, and having no brother, had inherited everything from her father upon his death. She had been well educated, and was better dressed than most of Jesus' followers. She wanted to talk to me at great length about the things I had seen and felt. She was not a young girl, but was still not old, and she had a quality about her that you had to sense, because it could not be seen with only the eyes. Her hair was dark and her skin very smooth and olive colored. Her eyes were not the usual brown, but were a blend of hazel and amber, and they seemed to be seeing into your inmost being when she looked at you. She had a full mouth with perfect lips, and was altogether a very beautiful woman.

As I spoke with Mary, we began to establish a rapport of sorts, a type of kinship that you usually feel with a sister. After I told her all that I could remember about all my sightings of Jesus, she began to tell me about herself.

"I was raised in a house just outside the village of Magdala, an only child of an aging father and middle-aged mother who had just about given up the hope of ever having a baby of their own. They rejoiced greatly at my birth, even though I was not the son that they had both hoped for. Nonetheless, my father saw to it that I had a good education, and when I grew old enough, allowed several suitors to visit and seek my hand in marriage. I never saw anyone that interested me, and by the time that my parents were getting more insistant about me accepting someone as a husband to take care of me, they both died, within two weeks of one another.

"Since I inherited their wealth, and was taught how to care for all their possessions, I managed to keep the vineyards running, and maintained all the sheep and goats as usual. I had many servants and hired hands to do the actual work. My life was peaceful, but also very boring. I grew so used to having my own way about everything that I must admit that I became an unpleasant person to be around. I thought only of myself, and spent money on clothes and perfumes. I never wanted to see poverty or misery around me, and closed my eyes to people who were having trouble just living from day to day.

"Then one day, everything changed. I was invited to supper at a house where I heard Jesus of Nazareth was staying, and I was interested in meeting him. As we reclined at the supper table, it seemed that everything Jesus said was directed at me in one way or another. At first, I felt my anger rising. After all, who was he to lecture me on how I should live? Finally, he looked straight into my eyes, and said, 'Mary, I see that you have been possessed by the seven devils of wealth, and your heart has been greatly hardened against your fellow men.'

"As I looked back at him, I actually lost myself in his eyes. I felt drawn deeply into them, and far out of my own self. I could see love, pity, compassion, sympathy, all those emotions that had become so foreign to me. Suddenly, I felt that I wanted to change. I threw myself at his feet, and asked if he could rid me of my burden. He placed his hands upon my head and prayed, and I felt my heart softening. My entire outlook on life changed in just that instant. I looked at him and felt such an onrush of love as I have never felt before for anyone. I begged him to let me be one of his followers.

"He told me the parable of the rich man trying to enter the kingdom of heaven. As the story ended, he explained to me that following him would involve great sacrifice. I felt that it would be worth any sacrifice, no matter how difficult, so I told him that I was ready. He said that I would need to consider the plight of the poor people, and how I could help them. As one of his followers, I would not be wealthy any longer, but living just as they did, from day to day, from the goodness and generosity of the people to whom he preached.

"Consequently, I sold all my property except the house. We all use that when we are in that area. Some widows with children live there all the time. All my wealth I distributed to the poor and especially to widows. The remainder of what I received at the sale of all my goods, I share with all these other followers that you see here. We all know how little value things of this world have, and only use what we need to survive. With all the demons of wealth driven out of me, I have felt such peace and joy in my heart, I cannot explain the wonder of it.

"I believed Jesus when he told us that he would die, but would rise again on the third day. Only his mother seemed to understand exactly what his words meant as he tried to explain to us that the scriptures would be fulfilled exactly as they were written by the prophets who knew of his coming for so many hundreds of years. I was still skeptical about the resurrection, though, because this is completely against every principle of nature that all human beings understand. Early this morning, I went to the tomb with some spices, to anoint his body if he was still there. I thought that I could talk the soldiers guarding the tomb into helping me roll away the stone.

"Instead, when I reached the cave with a couple of these other women, we didn't see any soldiers anywhere. We then saw the cave with the stone rolled away, and we thought that perhaps you had moved his body out and took it somewhere where none of us could find it. We looked into the tomb, and saw a young man dressed all in white, sitting at the end of the ledge where we had laid Jesus. He said, 'Why do you search for the living amongst the dead? He is not here—he has risen!' All of us were astonished at this, and we were told to go and tell his followers the good news. As we made our way back to the city, I lingered behind and noticed a gardener working. I asked him if he knew where Jesus was. He said, 'Mary!' I knew immediately that it was Jesus. Again, I threw myself at his feet and tried to throw my arms around him. He said, 'Mary, do not cling to me, because I have not yet ascended to my father.' Then he vanished. I came back here as fast as I could, and we all told these men what we had seen and heard. I told them that I had even seen and spoken to Jesus. None of them believed us, and Peter and John decided to go out and see for themselves. Now they have brought you back to us, and your story is even more amazing."

Hearing Mary relating all these things, I felt that I had known her for a long time. Somehow, she and I had shared in the most earth-shattering experience that a human being could have, that of seeing the crucified man coming back to life and walking and talking again. She and I talked at great length, comparing what each of us had seen, and filling each other in on details known only to us. Off and on during the day, the other men drifted by to listen to our conversation. Thomas continued to scoff, and finally, as the evening approached, he left to visit one of his relatives in the city.

Peter came to me and asked me to explain again about the rush of blood and water that came over Longinus and I from Jesus' side. I tried to convey all the feelings of that moment, and could not. Simple words could not express the depth of those emotions. Peter told me about the baptism of John, and I told him that I had been there to witness how he baptized Jesus. He said, "It seems that our Lord has greatly blessed you, to be able to observe so many meaningful moments in his life."

I then told him how I had been cured of an illness that should have killed me. I went on to relate the experience that Longinus had when his servant was also cured. Both these miracles took place without me or Marcellus ever having been near Jesus at the time. Peter pondered much over these revelations. He asked me many questions about how I felt. Was I sincere about not going back to the Roman military?

Did I have an earnest desire to change my life? Was I willing to talk about my experiences with others? Did I feel that my life had been forever altered, simply by all the things I had been through?

Apparently my answers to his questions satisfied him, because he finally stated, "I know that this is going to cause all kinds of problems with some of the others, but I truly feel that our Lord has sent you to us for a reason. I believe that you, above all of us, have been baptized by his very blood, and therefore have been singled out for some special purpose that we do not know yet, but will be revealed to us in time. Therefore, we will call you Mark Bar-Mathias, so your name will no longer sound Roman. You may stay with us and we will shelter you. If you desire, I will teach you all the things that Jesus taught us while you are with us."

I told Peter that I wanted to learn as much as I could about Jesus. He had touched my life on so many occasions, and some so miraculously, that I needed to know all about him. I wanted to dedicate my life to him, and promised that I would obey everything that Peter commanded of me. Satisfied at last, Peter made his announcement to the people in the room that I was now Mark Bar-Mathias, and would be one of them. Some of the men and women came to me and welcomed me into their group, while others still maintained their skepticism and distance, but that was exactly what Peter knew would happen.

Peter confided in me that, the night we had arrested Jesus, he had followed us to see what we would do. While he was waiting in the courtyard, some of the other people there pointed Peter out as a follower of Jesus, and he violently denied it. In fact, Peter stated that he had denied Jesus three times. Then he realized that it was exactly what Jesus had told him that he would do. He said if it took the rest of his life, he would always do penance for this terrible sin. And yet, he knew that Jesus understood and held no anger against him.

After we finished our evening meal, we all received a tremendous shock. Without a knock, without anyone unlocking or opening either of the doors, suddenly, there was Jesus standing in our midst. Most of the people were frightened and said, "It is a ghost." Peter fell on his knees and wept, and I felt tears streaming down my face as well. "Feel my hands and feet. I am not a ghost," Jesus grinned. "In fact, do you have anything to feed me? I am very hungry." The women hastened to bring Jesus some food, and he reclined and ate with us. Certainly no ghost could eat food as he was doing! After he finished eating, he told us that he had many things to do, and would see us several times again. He told us to stay in this place until we received further instructions. Then, just as suddenly as he appeared, he was gone. He just vanished.

As we all sat around discussing these marvelous things, we heard frantic knocking at the door downstairs. We heard the door creaking open, and the sound of footsteps on the stairs. Again at the landing, the knocking came again. Matthew went to the door and looked through the crack to make sure it was safe, then he opened it. In rushed two more men that the apostles seemed to know, and they were babbling excitedly. They were talking about having seen Jesus, in fact, walking with him on the road to Emmaus. They told us that they did not recognize him until they sat down to supper, and he blessed the bread and broke it. Then suddenly they knew it was Jesus, but before they could say anything, he disappeared.

Peter told them that we had all seen him, too. In fact, he had been here just a short while before, and we all knew that he was alive, even though many of us had seen him die. These men told us how Jesus explained the scriptures to them as they walked along the road, and how he had given them knowledge that they never found on their own while they studied. All the wisdom he had just taught them, they then began to impart to the rest of us. I was probably the only one in the room that knew practically nothing about their scriptures, but I still listened intently. I was anxious to learn all I could about this man, and all the predictions and prophecies that had been made about him, many of them hundreds of years ago.

It made perfect sense to me, given what I had personally experienced about Jesus, to learn that he was the living, human son of the God who made heaven and earth. It was difficult for me to grasp that there was only the one God, though. I had been raised in the Roman tradition, with multiple gods and goddesses, each one assigned to watch over specific areas in your life. That one God only could handle every aspect of your life was still something that I would need to really study over to accept. It was easy to think of Jesus as the son of a God, because of all the things that he did and said. I needed to work with Peter to learn more about this concept of only one God, and the covenant that He had made with the Hebrew people.

The Ascension

Over the next few weeks, I stayed in the upper room almost exclusively. At night, I would go out into the courtyard behind the house for fresh air and exercise. I spent my days studying everything I could about Jesus. I listened to stories told by Peter, Mary of Magdala, Matthew, John, and many of the others. I told Peter that I was having a problem with the concept of only one God, and he helped me through their Hebrew scriptures, so I could understand. He explained everything so thoroughly that it became easier to accept. Sometimes one of the others would tell me things that only they had experienced, and this also helped me tremendously.

Several times Jesus appeared to us again. The most notable time was the second time, when Thomas was with us. He had refused to believe us when we told him that Jesus had come to us. He continued to maintain that Jesus was dead, he was buried, and the work he had done had simply come to naught. He would not listen to any of our protestations. Therefore, it was almost amusing the next time Jesus came. As Thomas stood in total shock, Jesus walked over to him. As though he had heard exactly what Thomas had said about him, Jesus said, "Thomas, put your fingers in the holes in my hands and feet. Put your hand in my side, and know that it is indeed me." Thomas began to weep as he fell to his knees. Putting his head on the ground, he breathed, "My Lord and My God."

Jesus raised him up and embraced him. As he held him he comforted, "Blessed are you who have seen and have believed. But even more blessed are those who have not seen and have still believed." This made a big impact on my thoughts. It seemed that somehow the work he had begun was definitely going to continue, though I couldn't put those thoughts into words as yet. I had a vision of multitudes of men and women being taught and believing, and most of them were yet to be born. I felt a vague sense of what was being told to me to do, but couldn't formulate it then.

When the apostles decided to go fishing one evening, I stayed behind with the women. I was very happy to be able to talk with Mary, the mother of Jesus. She radiated such love and goodness that you just wanted to bask in it forever. Her beauty was so far beyond that of any other woman, there was no comparison. There was such a simple innocence surrounding her that it aroused all my protective feelings. While Mary Magdalene seemed to be totally self-sufficient, Mary projected a sense of total lack of self, and had no knowledge of how evil man could be, even though she had witnessed the terrible treatment of her son. I vowed that I would die before I would allow any harm to come to her.

Mary treated me as gently and lovingly as though I was her own son. She told me many things about Jesus' life in general, and how he grew from an infant to maturity. I learned that he had been trained by his foster father, Joseph, to be an expert carpenter. She told me all about how different he was from the other children that he played with, and how serious he always seemed to be about everything. I enjoyed listening to all her stories, and while the rest of the men were out fishing, I vowed that I would protect these women with my life, if necessary. The men first had to travel up to the sea of Tiberias and find some of Peter's family who were still fishermen. Then they would spend the greater part of the evening and the night out on the water, and bring in their catch in the morning. After skinning and preparing the fish, they would salt them and bring them back to Jerusalem to us. The trip would take them away for about 3 days, they estimated.

The time passed very swiftly for me, listening to the stories of the women, and learning so much about their beliefs, their scriptures and prophecies, and especially all about Jesus. We never knew when he would show up next, and he was never stopped or delayed by closed or even locked doors. It seemed that he had the ability to simply walk through them, or otherwise just to suddenly be there, without the necessity of walking anywhere. All this time, my beard was growing, and soon I began actually looking as authentic as a natural born Jew. I was fortunate that my hair was already black, and my skin was darkened by much exposure to the sun. With brown eyes, a beard, and a shawl covering my head, I would never be suspected by any Roman soldier. I had been in the country long enough to know Aramaic very well, and I also could speak Greek and Latin, due to my education. I was beginning to feel more comfortable every day in my new life as a Jew, and a follower of Jesus. Even more beneficial, as I found out during my studies, was that I had also been circumcised. As a child, I had developed some problems that our physician said could only be helped by circumcision. I could remember the pain and the discomfort for many days, and as I grew older, tried to hide it from the rest of the soldiers, because I knew this would be a source of ridicule from them. In my new life, it became a source of more acceptance from the followers of Jesus. To them, it was a sign that I had already made my covenant with God.

When the men returned from their fishing trip, they were bubbling over with excitement.

"We have seen the Lord again," Peter announced. He told us how disappointed they were when they had been in the boat all afternoon and night, and hadn't caught anything. They wanted so badly to bring us back some fish, and the trip seemed to have been a waste of time. As they came near the shore, they saw a man bending over a charcoal fire, cooking. He asked them if they had caught anything, and they said they hadn't. Then he told them to go back out and cast the net out the other side of the boat. When they did, they could scarcely haul in the number of fish in the net, and then they realized that it was Jesus on the shore. They rushed back to him with the boat almost capsizing for the weight of the fish, and Peter and John both jumped out and raced through the shallow water to embrace him.

Jesus seemed very happy, and had been cooking fish for their breakfast. He told them to add some of the fresh fish they had just caught, and they would all have a plentiful breakfast. They said it was like a celebratory feast, being with him like that again, and it was just like all the times they had traveled together. After they ate, he became serious and taught them more things that he said they needed to know for the future. Finally, once again, he disappeared, and the men returned to our place in Jerusalem with the fish after they had given some of them to Peter's family.

The men told us that Jesus informed them that his time on earth was just about over, and he would be returning to his father in heaven. He told us that the next time we saw him would be the last time, and to continue to wait at the house in Jerusalem for him. We all had mixed emotions at this news. I was sad because I had so briefly known Jesus. I envied his apostles for having had the experience of sharing those three years of travel and teaching with him. I felt that even if I lived with him for three years, I still wouldn't know everything there was to know about him.

For the next few days, we were all in quite a state of expectation. We were torn between wanting to see Jesus again, and knowing that it would be the last time. Everyone kept talking about all the lessons they had learned, and I continued to grow in my knowledge as I listened to all of them.

At last the morning came and Jesus was there. He looked happy and just a little sad too. He told us that he wanted us to gather a large crowd to see him go, and told us to meet him on top of a hill outside the Mount of Olives. For the first time, he came directly to me and spoke only to me. I was awestruck, and again mesmerized by the power of his eyes, and the depths they invited me into. He told me that he was charging me with the safety of his mother and John, whom he had ordered to be her son in his place. He told me that I would later understand the special task he had planned for me, and that I would never be killed in his service, though most of the others would. I couldn't even respond, I was so overwhelmed. Then he said that I was to accompany him and his mother to the hill, and I was overjoyed to be able to spend so much time in his company. The rest of the apostles had left to round up a large crowd, as Jesus had wanted, and said they would meet us on the hillside.

Jesus talked with us as we walked to the hill. He especially devoted a lot of time to his mother. The rest of us with him fell back a little to give him some private time with her, and they had their heads together during most of the walk. Soon we arrived at the place he had designated, and some people were already beginning to drift in, as the apostles had announced that Jesus was there. Jesus laughed and spoke with many of the people as they arrived, and within an hour, there was a crowd of around 500 people there.

When all the apostles had returned with the people they had called, Jesus signaled for quiet, and he spoke to us very seriously, as he said, for the last time. He told us that we were all commissioned to go out in the world and continue the teaching that he had started, to all the people in the world. He said he was going to his Father in Heaven, and would prepare a place there for all of us. He went to each one of his apostles and women who had followed him faithfully, and spoke to each individually. He embraced each one very lovingly. Even though he seemed radiantly happy, there was a tinge of sadness as he bid all his loyal friends farewell. When he came to me, I almost fainted as he took me into a loving embrace, as he had done with his closest friends. Words cannot describe the wonder of that touch.

We wondered what was going to happen, and how he would be leaving us. Soon, it became very clear, as he walked a slight distance away from us, to the crest of the hill. He stood there and held his arms up, and he began to glow. That is the only way I can describe it. The beautiful light came down to him, and also seemed to be coming from within him at the same time. Clouds began swirling around him, and we saw his feet leaving the ground. As we watched in breathless awe, he rose higher and higher, glowing ever brighter as he went up. Soon he disappeared into the clouds, and we all stood there gaping at the sky as though hoping to catch another glimpse of him. His last words to us continued to echo through our minds, "I will be with you till the end of time."

I looked at Mary, and it was almost impossible to imagine what she was feeling. She had a look of pride and joy on her face as she gazed upward, yet tears coursed down her cheeks. It seemed that she was extremely happy and yet emotionally devastated at the same time. She caught me looking at her, and she said, "He was a gift from God to me, especially, but he was also sent by God to be a gift to the entire world. I miss his physical presence, but I knew from the very beginning that he was only going to be with me until he felt the call to fulfill his father's will on this earth."

Then, two men dressed in dazzling white robes were just suddenly there, and they asked us, "Men of Galilee, why do you stand here looking at the sky? This same Jesus who has been taken up, will return in the same way, at the appointed time, and you will see him coming from the clouds."

After they had spoken to us, they too, disappeared, and we all stood there talking about what we had seen. Peter told us that he had some important news for us, and would tell us when we had all returned to the house. We knew Jesus was gone and there was no point standing there any longer, so we all returned to the house. As soon as we were back in the upper room, Peter told us what Jesus had explained to him. We were all to be gathered together in this place in 40 days' time. At that time, we were to receive something very special from God, and we would be told exactly what it was that we were all commissioned to do.

The Descent Of
The Holy Spirit

We spent the next weeks simply surviving. Every one of us was afraid. The apostles were fearful that, as former followers of Jesus, they might also be arrested and put to death. I was worried that somehow I would be discovered by the Romans, and I would also be put to death, with the exception being that I would be beheaded, not crucified, since I was a Roman.

I immersed myself in studying their sacred scriptures, so I could understand more of what Jesus was about and what his teachings meant. Peter was very kind to me, and trusted me completely. He told me that since one of Jesus' apostles had killed himself, there was an opening for one more. As a Gentile, most of the others were not ready to accept me in that position, but Peter said that Jesus had talked to him about it, and had great plans for me as well as each one of them. In order to do what Jesus had asked, I needed to know all about their religion.

The lessons began with Peter telling me about the covenant that God had made with the patriarch, Abraham. I listened with awe, as I pondered the deep faith the man must have had, in order to just pack up all his possessions, and go where God had told him. And also, how God had promised Abraham that he would be the father of countless generations to come. Even this Abraham believed, even though he was a man advanced in years, and his wife had long passed the child-bearing age. Eventually, how Sarah had borne a son, called Isaac, and how God had tested Abraham's faith when calling him to sacrifice that only son. And how God had truly blessed Abraham for his faith, and fulfilled his promise, and the sons of Abraham were the Jews.

Then followed the ancient history of the Israelites, as they called themselves. It was truly fascinating to me, especially since I was an avid student of history. I learned about all their ancestors, many of whom seemed to be almost supernatural in their deeds. Even the Hebrew women had their place in this history. Deborah, a judge of the people and also a fearless warrior. Judith, who had saved an entire area settled by the Israelites by using her faith in God. And Queen Esther, who had redeemed all her people by being in a time and place that allowed her to influence the king. I came to know very intimately all the descendents of Isaac, beginning with Jacob and Esau. How Jacob eventually became the father of twelve sons, who individually became the leaders of the twelve tribes of Israel. Then there was the story of Joseph, and how even though his brothers plotted to do away with him, was made the second in command to Pharaoh himself.

The story of Joseph especially appealed to me. I could truly identify with this young lad who had been torn from his home and sold into slavery in the land of Egypt. I marveled at his progress from slave to respected commissioner, second only to Pharaoh. In his position of power, he never lost faith in his God, and continued to pray and praise him for all the good things he did for Joseph. During the terrible famine that affected the entire country, Joseph's brothers traveled to Egypt to purchase food for their starving families. Joseph recognized them, but of course, they didn't know who he was. Joseph had become so powerful and adopted the customs and dress of the Egyptians that he was thought to be one of them.

The reunion of Joseph and his brothers was very touching to me, especially when his aged father Jacob came to see him. I missed my own father very much by this time, and I felt tears rolling down my cheeks as I visualized this emotional meeting. Eventually, Joseph's entire family moved to Egypt, and enjoyed life there until the Pharaoh died. The next Pharaoh wasn't too happy with the Israelites living in his country, and he eventually made them slaves. They lived in Egypt for hundreds of years in slavery, and were crying out to God to save them. Then God sent Moses to them to redeem them from their oppression.

Moses had been raised as the son of Pharaoh's daughter, so he was extremely well educated. He only became aware of his people's plight one day when he saw one of his fellow Israelites being beaten unmercifully by an Egyptian guard. Moses became enraged and killed the guard. Then, realizing what a dreadful crime that was, he fled into the desert. He married a Cushite woman and lived the life of a simple shepherd, until God called him to rescue the Jewish people. Reluctantly, he journeyed back to Egypt with his brother Aaron to plead with Pharaoh to let his people go. After much difficulty, and with a lot of help from God, who sent various plagues down to show Pharaoh that he wanted his people free, Pharaoh eventually did tell them to leave. This was only after the last terrible plague, when all the first born males of every household were struck dead in the night that the Jews now celebrate as Passover. So Moses led all the Hebrew people out of the land of Egypt toward the promised land, which was where they lived at this present time.

Peter explained how the customs and laws had been given to Moses, after he had rescued the Hebrew people from slavery in Egypt. How he had been called to Mount Sinai and actually spoken directly to God himself. How God had given specific instructions on how to build the Ark of the Covenant that he was making with the Israelites, as he called them. The story was fascinating, and I realized more each day how steeped in their faith these people were. Peter also explained that Jesus came to bring the new and everlasting covenant, which would then be with all people in the entire world. He didn't want his followers to be so concerned with all the countless rules and regulations and rituals that were outlined in Moses' laws. Jesus came to simplify our faith, and bring us all to an understanding that we needed only to believe in him and live our lives the way he taught us, and we would be with him forever in heaven.

Peter explained how powerful the Ark of the Covenant was. As a former soldier, I was very interested in the stories of all their battles. Even though many times they were badly outnumbered, as long as they carried the Ark into battle with them, they were always victorious. The Ark contained the tablets of stone on which God himself had inscribed the commandments. As the container for the Covenant God had made with his people, it was greatly revered. This is why the apostles loved Jesus' mother so much. She was considered to be a living Ark, having carried Jesus within her body for nine months. She was revered in the same way that the old Ark of the Covenant had been. Somehow, during the centuries, this Ark had disappeared, but Mary was still living, and Jesus had told us all he was bringing the new covenant to us. Mary herself was very humble about all this. She always maintained that it was God who had done the wonderful, miraculous things, and all she had done was be obedient to his wishes, as he asked all of us to be. Each day I learned more and more from her, as well as Peter and the other apostles, the ones who weren't so resentful of my presence, that is. Some of them still were very guarded around me, and they couldn't get over the fact that I was a former Roman soldier and had been instrumental in Jesus' capture and death.

Moses was considered one of the greatest prophets of the people, and he was called the Lawgiver, since he had presented the commandments from God to the Israelites. He had written the Torah that they studied and meditated on constantly. I studied this holy book and felt that I had been present at every event described there. In addition, with my studies in languages, I could see many things that were written in a way that you could only understand by study and meditation. Eventually, I seemed to forget all my old Roman ways and different gods, and fully and completely accepted that there was only Yahweh, the creator of the world and the only God. Jesus was sent miraculously to be His human son, born of a pure virgin. Yet he too, was God, being His son.

Finally the 40 days had passed, and every one of us in the inner group had gathered again in the upper room. We sat around talking and wondering what was going to happen. Many of the group came slinking in, still fearful of the crowds outside, and terrified that they would be found out as followers of Jesus. Most of the women were more bold, since they knew that because of their sex, they wouldn't be singled out for arrest. There was another festival going on in Jerusalem at that time, and large crowds of people were milling about through the streets, greeting each other and renewing friendships.

We were all talking quietly in the upper room, listening to the noise of the crowd outside. First we heard some commotion in the crowd, and then became aware of what they were talking about. We heard a very loud wind rushing down the streets, and the people outside were frightened at the sudden appearance of what seemed to be a violent storm. Then the wind stopped, and I cannot describe exactly what happened next, though I will try.

I felt the room tremble slightly, in just the same way the ground had trembled when Jesus was about to walk out of the tomb. As I registered this fact, I became aware of a tingling sensation building up all around me. I saw that the other men and women in the room were also experiencing some different sensations, according to the looks on their faces. Then I felt a warmth coming into my body, and my thoughts began racing wildly. I saw little flashes of fire coming down over everyone's heads, and judging from what I was feeling, there was also a flame over my head as well. Peter was seated opposite me, and he looked at me as I watched the flame dance over his head. Then it seemed to burn right into his skull, and disappeared. It also seemed that for a little while, everyone in the room had a glow about them.

Everyone began talking at once. Different voices came from all over the room, and I heard many things, like, "Now I know what the Lord has determined for me to do." "I understand so much now, that I never did before." "What marvels are appearing in my thoughts now." "I need to go and do what I have been ordered." And many other such statements. At the same time, I felt that I had been given much knowledge. As Jesus had promised me, I was certain of what it was he wanted me to do. I felt that he had singled me out as a Gentile, to more accurately carry his word to people who were outside the Jewish faith. I cannot explain where this feeling of certainty came from, but it was as solid as if Jesus himself had stood there and commanded me to do this. I could see that everyone else had received the same kind of certainty, and they had a fire within them that I had not seen previously.

Peter said, "The Lord has told me to carry his teaching to all nations, and to begin in this city." Others began to agree with him, and we all felt compelled to go out into the crowd and begin our preaching. We stood among the people and spoke to them, one at a time, about Jesus and what he taught. I noticed the crowd staring at us strangely, and realized as they talked among themselves, that no matter what language we spoke, they could understand us as if we were speaking in their native tongue. Even though I was still very new to the Jewish beliefs, I had learned so much about Jesus' teachings, that I, too, told the story to them as I had been taught. I spoke in Aramaic, because I didn't want to use Latin and attract the attention of the Roman soldiers who were watching the crowd. Even so, people from all over the world were gathered there and every one of them had no trouble understanding me.

This was a far different group of people from the ones who had gathered in that room for so long now. Where before they had been timid and fearful, now they were bold and courageous in proclaiming their faith. I seemed to understand with the new knowledge that I had been given, that we had all been visited by the very Holy Spirit of God Himself, and he had put all the things inside us that we would need to carry out his will. Along with the courage I felt, I also had firm convictions about the teaching that Jesus had brought, and I knew that I had enough knowledge as a gift from this Spirit, that I could teach others just as well as the apostles had been teaching me. From that moment on, we stopped fearing arrest and punishment, and became fearless and bold.

Proclaiming The Covenant

All of us were filled with a zeal that cannot be explained. We continued to preach to the crowds every day. Peter and most of the others went into the Synagogues, but this was something that I was not allowed to do, even though I looked the same as the rest. With my new wisdom, I understood that I would be teaching outside the Jewish beliefs, and I could speak more easily to Gentiles, being one myself, as they considered me to be. We traveled in groups of three to six people, going to all the towns and villages and speaking to anyone who would listen to us.

The very first day when all of us spoke, preached, or otherwise taught the words of Jesus, we had thousands of people inspired enough to beg us for baptism. This was encouraging, since with each conversion, we were given more and more credibility. It was actually a lucky thing for me that they did not allow me to teach in their synagogues, because after so many people began listening to them and being baptized, the high priest and his temple guards began arresting the teachers. Many of them were hauled before the Sanhedrin and charged with blasphemy. Several of them were beaten and some were put in prison.

One day, some of the new converts came to us with a look of fear and apprehension on their faces. They told us that Peter himself had been arrested and put in a prison cell with chains on his arms and legs. John and a few other apostles were with him. All of us gathered together and prayed to Our Lord for deliverance and for safety for Peter and his group. All during that night, I kept waking up and praying for them. I slept very restlessly, and felt guilty about even the sleep that I got, because I knew that those in prison would not have been getting any sleep while they were in chains.

Early in the morning, there was a light knock on the door. The man assigned to guard the door opened the peephole to see who was there. He became very animated and excited, and fumbled with the latch as he tried to open the door. He made so much noise that all of us in the room were awake by the time the door opened. We were dumbfounded when we saw Peter, John, and the others walk in calmly. They sat down after greeting us and asked for something to eat. Then Peter began to relate the most incredible story.

"The priests told me that I had to stop teaching about Jesus. I answered that I could not stop talking about him, and they decided to put me in prison. I was beaten and then chained into a cell without food or water. I spent the evening and early night in prayer and contemplation of all that we had gone through with Jesus, and suddenly I was almost blinded by a light. I thought it was the jailers coming to torture me again, but instead I felt a flood of peace and love, and knew that this was something coming from Jesus. I could see that it was an angel, and he just pointed to our chains and they fell off. I stood up, and then the doors to our cells opened. The angel motioned us to follow, and we walked right through the prison, past the guards and outside with no alarm. Even the dogs outside did not bark. I was told to go and continue talking just as I had been doing, and so here I am."

Naturally all of us were deeply impressed by this story. It was certainly divine intervention that brought Peter and his associates out of the depths of the prison. We felt reassured by the knowledge that God Himself was working through us and with us, and offering His protection against all humans who were against us.

In the next few months we all continued to teach and convert many hundreds to follow in the teachings of Jesus. Peter especially seemed to have been blessed above the rest, by being able to perform miracles of healing in the name of Jesus. He was constantly getting into trouble with the priests because of this. All of us were punished, captured, imprisoned, threatened, or otherwise intimidated to make us stop teaching these new, radical ideas. Of course, none of their threats stopped us, and we continued to grow and thrive. We sometimes met at local homes and celebrated together as Jesus had taught the apostles on the night before his death. He told us that the bread was now no longer bread, but was his body, which was given up for us. The wine was now no longer wine, but his blood which would be shed for all of us in the new and everlasting covenant. He had told his disciples that whoever ate his body and drank his blood would have life everlasting. We re-created this ritual in every one of the house meetings that we had. I was allowed to participate in these rites, since they were not conducted in the synagogue. Each time I spoke or taught about Jesus, my faith was strengthened further. I was beginning to understand exactly how my life had been given to me just for the purpose of following Jesus. All the events in my entire life were like signposts pointing to the eventual goal that I was to reach. I began to feel such a fierce love for Jesus that I cannot describe or explain it. It was as though the flames of the Holy Spirit that I had received on that one day, had remained within my being, and were being fanned into a total burning, all consuming blaze.

One of our new converts was a young man named Stephen. He stayed with us for several days, learning all he could about Jesus. He had been in the room on the day when the fires of God came upon all of us, including him. He was one of our most eloquent speakers, in spite of his youth, and he was fearless and courageous in the face of all the threats we all constantly received. We received word that a Pharisee named Saul was desperately attempting to stamp out our movement. He was extremely radical, and being well educated, could also speak very convincingly and brilliantly. His threats were actually causing some of the people who had been baptized to recant and renounce the teachings of Jesus. Saul convinced them that we were heretics and would cause them all to be damned for eternity if they continued to follow us.

Stephen continued to go out into the marketplace where the crowds were gathered every day, and tell his story. One day he bumped into Saul as he spoke. Saul challenged him and tried to debate with him, showing his knowledge of the scriptures. Stephen stood up bravely and countered everything that Saul said with something that Jesus said to refute that. Saul became frustrated and angry, and finally he told the men in the crowd that this was a heretic and blasphemer, and he should be stoned to death.

The men took Stephen outside the city, and Saul held their cloaks as they gathered stones. Stephen demanded his right to speak before he died, and he spoke eloquently. He began by going back to the ancient prophets and Moses, bringing them step by step to the fulfillment of all the prophecies, which was the birth and ministry of Jesus. He lifted his eyes and with a look of ecstasy on his face, said, "Behold, I see the heavens now, and I see Jesus on the throne, waiting to welcome me!" With that, the first stone was cast, and Stephen fell to his knees. He uttered no sound except to call on Jesus to welcome his spirit, and the stones just rained on him, long after he was dead and all the blood had run out of his body. All of us were thoroughly shaken by this event, because we could see that following Jesus could actually result in our persecution and death. But hadn't Jesus warned all of us about this? He told us that we would suffer, and many would be put to death in his name, but we must persevere, and then our rewards in heaven would be great. I kept remembering that Jesus had told me that I would not be killed, but many of the others would. This was only the beginning.

We began traveling to different places where many of the Jews had been scattered over the years, teaching in their synagogues and market places. Everywhere that we went, persecution followed us. Every one of us, including myself, was thrown into various prisons at least once. We all experienced miraculous releases from these prisons too, which reinforced our determination to obey Jesus, since he was clearly working on our behalf from wherever he was. Saul became one of the worst of the tormentors. He was almost maniacal in his quest to stamp us and our movement from the face of the earth. He too began traveling where we went, trying to stop us before we got too many converts.

We traveled to Damascus on one of these trips. One of our communities had called upon us to return and help them, so several of us traveled there together. Mary Magdalen and Mary, Jesus' mother, were with our group, to help with the women's part of the community work. Jesus had commissioned us to help the poor, especially the widows and orphans who were totally dependent upon others for their lives. Those converts who had money and property, as Mary Magdalene had, usually sold their holdings and gave their money to the apostles to be divided into shares for these poor people. It was Jesus' desire that all of us should love one another and look out for one another, and we took all his teaching very seriously. We eventually assigned one trustworthy man in each area to dispense the necessary items from the treasury to the needy.

We stayed at the home of a man named Ananias in Damascus. He was a very devout man, dedicated to a life of serving the Lord. He welcomed us into his home and guided us to the homes in the town where the community met. We taught and shared our experiences with this group, and reinforced their desire to follow the teachings of Jesus. The more I taught about his teachings, the more perfect I found them to be. If everyone on the earth followed Jesus' teachings, there would be no poverty, no war, no mistreatment of anyone. In fact, it would be a perfect world.

After we had been in Damascus for a few weeks, we had a bad shock. There came a knock at the courtyard door one day, and a voice asking if this was the house of Ananias. Ananias went to the door and said this was his house, and the voice asked to be let in. A servant opened the door, and there stood some soldiers leading a horse on which there sat an obviously blind man. To our horror, we saw that the man was Saul! Had he followed us here with the object of putting all of us to death? Various thoughts flitted through our minds, but then we heard Saul speak. "I was directed by the Lord to come to this house. His voice told me that if I came here and listened to you, I would be cured." We were even more astounded when Ananias replied, "I was told by the Lord in a vision that you would come here, and I was directed to pray over you and cure you." The soldiers helped Saul down from his horse, and he knelt on the ground. We watched as Ananias placed his hands on Saul's head and lifted his eyes to heaven and prayed. As we watched, we saw flecks of things like fish scales fall out of Saul's eyes onto the ground. He stood up and happily announced that he could see again, and Ananias invited him to stay and eat.

Nervously, we all sat as far away from Saul as we could, but Ananias and Mary seemed to have no fear of him. They asked him to tell us what happened, and when he did, it was almost too strange to believe. If I hadn't already seen so many miracles happening in the name of Jesus, I wouldn't have believed it either. Saul told us he was riding toward Damascus to try and eradicate the followers of Jesus there. At this, instead of his usual pride and arrogance, he seemed embarrassed and ashamed. All of a sudden, a very bright light shone down on the travelers. Saul's horse reared in fright, and Saul himself was knocked off the horse onto the ground. He looked up and in the midst of the light, he heard a voice imploring, "Saul, Saul, why are you persecuting me?" Other things were told to him, but he was struck totally blind. The voice, which Saul now knew to be the voice of Jesus, told him to continue to Damascus and seek out a man there named Ananias.

"So, here I am," Saul continued, "And I don't know what to make of all this. I was blind, and now once again I see. My heart has changed drastically too, because I no longer feel as I once did. I need to follow the orders I was given that day on the road, to seek you out, not as enemies, but as friends and brothers." Mary went to Saul and embraced him as lovingly as though he was her son. She welcomed him to our midst in the name of her son, Jesus. She seemed to be the first one of us to grasp what had happened to Saul. Ananias too, though he first seemed skeptical, had already realized that God worked in many mysterious ways, and we needed to trust him.

Gradually, as the days went by, and we all talked with Saul, we came to believe that he had been stricken by God, and healed by God for a specific purpose, as all of us had, at one time or another. He seemed as eager now to learn about Jesus as he had been to persecute the followers of Jesus. All of us taught him, shared our experiences with him, and for a strange reason that I could not begin to fathom, I found myself confessing to him that I was a defected Roman soldier, and subject to beheading if I were ever to be caught. He seemed unfazed by any of our stories, comparing them to what he had experienced himself. He begged to be baptized so that he would bear witness to the truth of Jesus' teachings. As one of the church elders, Ananias baptized him in the name of Jesus. He then laid his hands on Saul's head and prayed for the Holy Spirit to come down upon him. We watched in amazement as a fiery flame descended from heaven and hovered over Saul. It flamed into a glowing nimbus around Saul's entire head, and then seemed to disappear inside him.

Saul had a look of complete ecstasy on his face. He stood as if in a trance for several minutes, and we waited expectantly for him to speak with us. His eyes shone with a flashing intensity, yet he appeared not to see any of us. It was as though only his body stood there, while his spirit was somewhere else. At last, he seemed to come back to his senses. He shook his head and looked at us as though he had been gone for a long time. He told us that God's Holy Spirit had actually been communing with him, and giving him specific instructions as to what he was to do. Since we had all felt this same way when the Holy Spirit visited us, we knew exactly what he was talking about.

Saul said that God had instructed him to learn from us about Jesus and his Way to Life. Then he was to travel to Jerusalem and meet with Peter. God had told Saul that, as Peter had been chosen to be the leader of his church, Saul was to go out into the world and gather all the souls that he could, to be baptized and follow Jesus. Peter was first concentrating on converting Jews, but Saul, as a Roman citizen and world traveler, was to devote his preaching mainly to the Gentile peoples.

One day Saul announced that he no longer wanted to bear that name. Instead, he would change it to the Roman version and now be known as Paul. After he learned everything we could teach him, he also began to go to the synagogues with the disciples, and he preached fiery sermons on Jesus behalf. Many of the people there could not believe it either. They began by being hostile and aloof when Paul appeared. Then they started to marvel at the way he was teaching on Jesus' behalf. We could hear them muttering amongst themselves, "Isn't this the man who was so intent on stamping out all the people who were following Jesus?" But as time went on, every one who heard Paul could see that he too, was burning inside with the Holy Spirit. We could see that God had indeed chosen wisely, since Paul was extremely well educated, a Roman citizen as well as a Jew, and was very eloquent, both in speech and in writing.

Paul And Luke

Soon Paul realized that it was time to return to Jerusalem and have Peter pray with him. He greatly desired to compare notes with him, and offer his help in spreading the wonderful news of Jesus' new covenant to all the Gentile countries. He requested that all of us travel with him, and his thirst for learning everything about Jesus could not be quenched. He sought me out in particular, and said that, as a Gentile myself, I could be of great help to him as he carried the words of Jesus to all the countries in the world.

Consequently, we all traveled back to Jerusalem and met with Peter. He too, was very suspicious and withdrawn at first. Paul knelt at his feet and asked him if he would lay his hands on him and pray for the gifts of the Holy Spirit to continue to burn within him. After all of us had discussed everything that we had personally witnessed about Paul's conversion, Peter reluctantly agreed. He raised his eyes to heaven and prayed, as he placed his hands on Paul's head. "Dear

Lord and Master, if this servant has indeed been chosen by you for your work, please let your Holy Spirit come upon him as it has on all the rest of us."

Soon, a bright light seemed to travel from Peter's hands right into Paul's head. Paul began speaking a language that none of us could understand, but Peter seemed to know what he was saying. The air around Paul seemed to pulsate and glow for a few minutes, just as it had when the tongues of fire came down on all of us. Finally, he seemed to come back to himself, and we could see that he was simply burning with excitement and desire to get to work. We thought he had been filled with the Spirit before, but this was magnified now to such an intensity that it was almost unbelievable.

Paul told Peter that he would be forever mourning the followers that he had punished and killed. He said that a lifetime of working for Jesus couldn't begin to take away his guilt, but he was devoting his life to God anyway, trusting in His forgiveness. Peter told Paul that he understood completely, that he himself had even denied knowing Jesus when the soldiers had arrested him. That he was ready to die of sorrow for what he had done. Then he was comforted by a vision, that Jesus had already forgiven him before he had even denied him. Jesus himself reinforced that fact after his death and resurrection, when he told Peter that he still wanted him to be the foundation of his church, and he trusted him with the keys to his kingdom.

Since John was planning to stay in Palestine preaching in some of the smaller villages, he told me that I should accompany Paul on his missions to reach the world. John insisted that Mary would be safe with him until I returned, and I could once again be their protector.

We sat hunched over maps for the next few days, plotting our travels so that we would be able to reach the major cities to spread the word. In the beginning, since Jesus had told his apostles that he was the Way, the Truth, and the Life, his followers called themselves believers in the Way. "Do you follow the Way?" became one of the best questions we used when meeting strangers, to determine if they were followers or not. In this way, we went to quite a number of cities, gathering more and more believers everywhere we went.

Soon, we had quite a large group traveling in our party. Paul had taken a special interest in a young man named Timothy, and looked on him as though he was his own son. He taught Timothy so that he would be prepared to also go out on his own and continue to convert as many to the Way as possible. Paul had a special talent for picking out men and women who were especially capable of being leaders. He established churches in many of the follower's homes. Due to the breaking of the bread that Jesus had told his apostles to continue to do in order to follow him, the Way followers could not worship in the synagogues. In addition to this, most of our converts were not Jews but Gentiles. We were getting Greeks, Romans, Syrians, and many others to follow the Way.

Paul had plans to travel as far away as remote Gaul, where Caesar had traveled and conquered, and written many stories about. Most of the people were completely pagan, worshiping many gods, as I had been raised to do. It was Paul's desire to reach all of them and convert them to follow Jesus only, as the son of the only God and being a part of God. It was inspiring to me to watch and listen to him as he preached, exhorted, demanded, explained, and taught all the things that Jesus had brought to our earth. In many cases, I also preached and taught, omitting only that I was a former Roman soldier. This could have been my death sentence, and it was still much safer for me to continue my masquerade as a Jew who had been converted to the Way. I built up more and more confidence each time I spoke to the people. It was heart-warming to see how the words reached down into people's hearts, and how they begged for baptism and conversion.

On one of our travels, we met another distinguished man. He was a physician, and said that his name was Lucius (in the Roman language), and so we called him Luke. He had lived and studied in Greece, where he had proved what an accomplished physician he was. When he found that we had been staying in Mary's house in Nazareth, the very house that Jesus lived in for almost 30 years, he asked Paul if I could be spared to accompany him and take him there. He had already been converted to the Way, and said that he wanted to find out as much as he could about Jesus and his teaching.

Paul said that I was no longer needed there, and I had proven that I was a convincing speaker, and could probably be better used in Palestine. He was gathering such a crowd of believers that they would be able to take my place. It was a rapidly spreading movement, which was yet another indication of how Jesus' teaching reached into everyone's hearts. I bid Paul, Timothy, and the others a tearful farewell, and Luke and I prepared to return to Judea.

Our trip was uneventful, even though we passed through many areas where bandits roved and preyed on travelers. It seemed that we were under the special protection of God, and we never felt any real danger. We went all the way down to Nazareth, since John had told us that he was taking Mary back there. I still felt a small fluttering of apprehension every time a group of Roman soldiers came near, but I was never challenged.

We arrived at Mary's house late one afternoon, hot and dusty. Mary Magdalene was staying there too, and washed our feet to help refresh us. Then they brought us food and wine, and we rested in the shade of the courtyard.

Luke told Mary who he was, and how he had such a burning desire to learn all about Jesus. He told her that he had been given a vision and was instructed to write things down for future generations to read. Mary already seemed to know all these things, and I am certain that she had many more revelations from God than all the rest of us put together. She invited Luke to stay with her for a week or two, or however long he needed, and she would relate everything that she could remember to him.

For the next several days, we spent most of our time in the shaded courtyard outside the house, where the breeze was cool and it was more comfortable than being inside. Mary told Luke everything about Jesus' life, even from the first announcement to her that she was to be his mother. I was astonished at the calm way she talked about visits from angels, as though it was an everyday occurrence. She had been a very young virgin when she first received a visit from the angel who called himself Gabriel. Not only had he told her she would be the Mother of the Son of the Most High, but her aged relative, Elizabeth, had also conceived a son. These were some of the most remarkable things I had ever heard, and I could almost see the events unfolding before my eyes, as Mary spoke of them.

I then realized that John the Baptist, whom I had seen and talked to on the day Jesus was baptized, was the son of this woman who had been long past child-bearing years, "For nothing is impossible to God," as Mary related. We heard the story of how Joseph, who had been betrothed to Mary, was ready to put her away quietly when he learned of her pregnancy. How an angel had then come to him as well, to explain that Mary had not sinned, that she was carrying the Holy One of God, and Joseph had been chosen to be her spouse and protector.

We also heard the story of the long and painful trip to Bethlehem, when Mary was in the advanced stages of her pregnancy. Caesar Augustus had ordered the census to be taken, so Joseph and Mary both, as descendents of the great King David, had to go to his city, Bethlehem, to be counted. As they drew near the city, Mary felt the first pangs that the child was very soon to be born, and Joseph frantically tried to find a place for them to stay. In the end, there was no vacant room to be had anywhere in the city, but a kind innkeeper's wife had directed them to a stable where they would at least find shelter. It was then that Mary described something very strange, but what also made perfect sense to me.

"Joseph led our donkey to the stable, and I could see that it was a cave, hewn out of the side of a hill. You cannot imagine the feelings going on within me at that time; how the son of the Most High should not be brought into the world in such poor surroundings. Yet, as I reflect now on the events of Jesus' entire life, it was very symbolic. It was really after his death that I began to see the logic in all of it. Jesus, as the Son of God, came into the world in a cave in the earth. In a way, Jesus emerged from the earth that he created with his Father, to bring salvation to the entire world. Upon his death, once again he was laid in a tomb, which was a cave carved into the side of a hill. He brought himself back to life once again, and emerged again from a cave in the earth, bringing the hope of eternal life to all his people on earth. He came into the world first, being born in a cave, and he came into the world a second time after he conquered death, again from a cave. In this way, everything seems to fall into place for me."

Luke and I were both astounded at the manner in which Mary had put all these things into perspective. John, too, was amazed and listened to everything she said as attentively as Luke and I. Luke wrote many notes as she continued to relate the story of Jesus' life. How he had learned the trade of a carpenter under Joseph's tutelage. How he would sometimes seem to be in another world, even when surrounded by people. How he wanted to remain in the temple, debating with the priests, even at a very young age. How he took care of Mary when Joseph died. Mary had a brother with three children, and he helped see that she had enough to eat.

All too soon, the time came when Jesus told Mary that it was time for him to go out into the world and bring the news from God to all the people. He told her that he needed to fast and pray and when he was spiritually prepared, he would begin what he was sent here to do. He began by going to his cousin John to be baptized, then went into the hills and fasted and prayed for 40 days. I felt particularly honored that I had been present to witness with my own eyes, this baptism by John. When Jesus came out of the hills, he was thin and drawn, but seemed to have an inner fire that could not be quenched. He had begun preaching and gathering many people into his midst. He selected 12 men to be his closest disciples, and he called them apostles.

The men that Jesus had chosen seemed to be a mis-matched group from the beginning. There were some fishermen, a tax collector, and farmers among their group. Knowing how Jews felt about tax collectors, I marveled at how well they all got along. Matthew was the one whom they had the most difficult time accepting, but under Jesus' guidance, he soon became like a brother to them. John was the youngest, slightly more than a boy, and it made me wonder how Jesus could possibly look at some of these men and determine that they would make perfect leaders to help spread his teachings.

Mary told us that many women also joined the group, and she herself had traveled quite a bit with Jesus. She watched as Mary Magdalene experienced her conversion, and welcomed her into the group as a sister. There were Martha and Mary of Bethany, with their brother Lazarus, who always had a place for them to stay as they passed through that area. In fact, Jesus had seemed to carry a deep love for Lazarus, even though he hadn't chosen him to be one of his apostles. When word came that Lazarus was ill, Jesus said he would go to see him, but did not get started for a few days. When they finally arrived in Bethany, Jesus was told that Lazarus had died. Jesus wept at this news, but told the sisters that he would rise again.

Lazarus had been in the tomb for four days, and it was the heat of the summer. The Jews believed at that time that the soul could linger around the body for three days, but after that, the soul had completely departed, and the body was totally dead. When Jesus commanded that the stone be removed from Lazarus' tomb, everyone protested. "It has been four days, Lord, and the body has certainly begun to decay in this heat. Please, it will be too unpleasant." But Jesus insisted, and so a few of the men reluctantly rolled away the stone. Jesus looked up to heaven and prayed for awhile, then called for Lazarus to come out of the tomb. It almost caused total panic for the entire crowd, as they saw the wrapped body of Lazarus walk out of the tomb, with no smell of decay or anything other than the funeral wrappings to indicate that he had been dead. Word of this spread through the town like wildfire, and this is what made the temple priests so unhappy. Jesus was doing things that they could not do, and they were worried about losing their positions of authority and consequent luxury, if the people followed Jesus.

Mary continued with everything she could remember about Jesus. Luke told us that he had been told in a vision that the second coming of Jesus would not take place as soon as the apostles had originally thought. It would be some time before that happened, and Jesus wanted his teachings to be written down, so that future generations would have his words to study. I couldn't help but think back to the time when Jesus appeared to all of us when Thomas was present, and how he had said, "Blessed are you who have seen and believed. Blessed even more are those who have not seen and yet have believed." I wondered just how many generations it would take before Jesus returned as he had promised all of us at his ascension. His words would be written down so that all people in the future, no matter how long it took, would have his teachings to follow. Those people would certainly be well blessed by Jesus, having not seen him, but believing in him as they read his words.

Finally, Luke had received all the information from Mary that he needed. He said he would talk to all the other apostles who had lived with Jesus for the three years of his ministry, and convince them that they, too, should write down all they could think of about Jesus and his teachings. Some of the apostles could not read or write, but they could relate their stories to scribes, and the stories would be preserved that way.

Before Luke left to journey toward Ephesus where Paul was currently preaching, Mary said she wanted to show us something very important. She insisted that we come inside the house, because she did not want anyone else to catch so much as a glimpse of what she wanted to uncover. Wondering greatly about this, Luke, John, and I all went into the house to see what Mary had. She rummaged around in a cupboard at the floor, well into the recesses, and brought out several objects. When I saw what they were, my breath caught and I felt my heart begin to pound. Tears welled up in my eyes, and I could hardly stand.

"Here is the spear that was used to determine that Jesus was truly dead," Mary said, as she held out the very spear that I had seen last in the hands of Longinus. I knew he had flung it away from him in disgust after he and I had experienced that mystical baptism of Jesus' blood and water. I did not know that one of the apostles had picked it up and given it to Mary. "Here is the horrible crown that the soldiers put on Jesus' head," Mary continued. She held out the circlet of thorny vines, hardened and discolored by the blood of Jesus. Next, she showed us the cup that Jesus had used at his final meal, when he told his apostles that this was to be the cup of his blood, of the new and eternal covenant, and all his believers should drink it in memory of him. Peter had brought that and given it to Mary. She next brought out the burial shroud that had remained in the tomb after Jesus had returned to life. It was stained with blood, but had been lovingly folded and kept ever since his death. Another object was very startling. It was a simple towel, but there was a perfect picture on it of Jesus' face. Mary explained how this came to be. "One of the women felt such compassion for Jesus as he struggled with his cross on the way to Golgotha, that she ran through the circle of soldiers and gently wiped Jesus' face. She was able to give him a couple of sips of water, too, before the soldiers whipped her out of the way. She brought the towel to me later that night, as I sat mourning and shocked at all the horrible things I had seen done to my beloved son that day. She was amazed to see the perfect image of his face imprinted upon it."

I was thoroughly shocked. Most of these objects I had personally seen on that horrible, never to be forgotten day. I remembered the young woman inching through the crowd with some water and a towel, lovingly pressing the towel to Jesus' face to clear the blood and sweat from his eyes. I also remembered the hatred and disgust I felt toward the soldier who had whipped her. I could hardly restrain myself from knocking him to the ground. All the events of that day came vividly to my mind once again, and it was amazing, but seeing the objects themselves, it was almost like receiving a blessing. I poured out all my feelings to Mary, and Luke listened in fascination. The last thing that Mary had kept was a piece of wood, blood-stained, that she said Jesus' feet had rested on as he hung on the cross. She said that she was told to keep these things until the day when she would be given instructions for their disposal. Then she returned them to their hiding place.

Luke also pressed me for every detail that I could remember about that day, and about the resurrection of Jesus. I went over and over it again and again, and still could not understand why I had been given such a blessing, to be able to witness the actual emergence from the tomb by the man I had seen die so horribly days before. Luke said he thought it was to give me the faith I needed for the duty I would be assuming, that of being an apostle to the Gentiles. I felt that Luke was right, because I had already spent the past year preaching with Paul and some of the other apostles. I had even been thrown into prison a couple of times in different places, and warned to stop teaching about Jesus. Like Peter and the rest of the men, I could not stop talking about Jesus, and was willing to risk imprisonment, torture, and even death as Steven had, before I would stop.

Luke found a caravan that he could join for greater safety, as he began his trip to meet Paul. He told us that he would not see us again on this earth, but would meet again in heaven one day, and with tearful embraces, we all parted with him.

Mary's Farewell

Over the next few years, I remained mostly with the numerous churches Paul, Luke, and Peter had been establishing all over the known world. They would preach, baptize, and teach, converting all who wanted to follow in Jesus' Way. Then they would move on to another province, leaving the infant churches in the care of those of us who had known Jesus intimately, and whom they could trust to continue teaching the truth.

In those early days, there was a lot of confusion. Since Jesus had been a Jew, there were many Jewish people who thought that Gentiles should be totally excluded from this faith. The only exception would be if they were willing to convert to Judaism, which involved many things, the hardest of which was their insistence that all men had to be circumcised before they could be accepted as a follower of Jesus. It seems a small thing to talk about, but imagine the abhorrence that a grown man felt being told that he had to undergo this painful operation. Many men turned away and gave up, but Paul and Peter continued traveling back and forth to try and find a middle ground. Peter finally agreed, after he had been given a dream several days in a row, that Jesus had truly desired that people of every race were to be given the chance at salvation, and that circumcision was one of the many things in the old covenant that no longer applied.

When this controversy died down, others sprouted up. Men began to come forward insisting that they had been given visions from the Lord, and they tried preaching in a distorted manner. We were kept very busy in those days, examining all who claimed to be prophets of Jesus, and putting incorrect teachings out of our little groups. It helped a great deal that those of us usually left in charge of these groups were either those of us who had directly known and heard Jesus for ourselves, or those who were thoroughly indoctrinated by Paul or Peter or one of the other apostles who had known Jesus.

In addition to keeping the teachings true, we were all subject to varying forms of persecution as well. I was beaten twice and thrown into prison three times. John was with me on two of those occasions, and we heard about others in our groups who had suffered even more. Many of us experienced miraculous releases, when angels would move amongst us and free us from our chains. Other times, natural events would work in our favor, as when an earthquake rolled through one of the towns and caused the jail walls to crumble and release us. None of us could truly grasp why so many were so drastically against us spreading the teachings of Jesus, especially when, if everyone followed those teachings, life would be far better in this world. We even heard of some of our numbers in different places being stoned to death or killed in other ways.

I remember one time when the priests were especially infuriated at us for teaching the Way of Jesus. One very wise man by the name of Gamaliel had approached them and told them that if our teaching was truly from God, there was nothing they could do about it, and it would not die down. If it was from man, as so many other beliefs had been, it would die of its own accord. Punishment and torture would have no affect on a divinely authored institution. We were startled at the wisdom of this man, and not surprised when he sought us out after our release from prison. He wanted to hear everything we could tell him about Jesus, and after listening and debating with us, he begged us to baptize him as well and accept him into our group. This sort of thing happened very often, that sometimes those who set out to stop our preaching, somehow became our most solid supporters.

Luke had been correct about my never seeing him again. Even though I occasionally managed to be in the same place as Paul, it seemed that Luke was somewhere else, even though he traveled mostly in the company of Paul or Peter. I kept track of him through many letters, though. He had written once that he was highly elated when one of his patients had been converted. This was a young man who lived with his widowed mother, and she too became a convert. Some time later, this young man became very ill, and Luke said that he had died. Luke laid his hands on him, and prayed in the name of our Lord Jesus, and the man sat up and appeared totally normal once again. Luke was overjoyed at this indication of Jesus' blessing on him and his efforts, and he became even more dedicated to spreading the good news of Jesus and his salvation. The young man who had been brought back to life also was burning with zeal to tell everyone he could talk to about his miraculous restoration. Those who had seen him lying lifeless were convinced that some awesome heavenly power had been at work. Events of this nature continued to pour in through letters and word of mouth, and it inspired all of us to renew our efforts in winning men to Jesus.

Mary sometimes traveled with us, especially to some of the nearer points in our journeys. John would always be with her at those times, and he and I became very close, as though we were brothers brought forth from Mary's womb. We had many discussions about Jesus, and I marveled at the strength and courage of John, the only one who had remained steadfast at the foot of the cross on that dreadful day. He was the youngest of the entire group, yet displayed a maturity far beyond what the rest had demonstrated on that day. He seemed to have a deeper understanding of some of the things that Jesus taught. Mary also talked to both of us about the love Jesus had for all mankind.

As the years went by, and I grew to know all the men who had been closely associated with Jesus, I also understood his teachings more and more thoroughly. John grasped how deeply Jesus loved everyone, and how he tried to stress to all his disciples that love was so very important. He even went so far as to say that the 10 commandments that had been given to Moses as a law for the Hebrew people could be summarized in two. Those two would be to love God with all your heart, mind and being, and to love your neighbor as you loved yourself. The more I pondered over these statements, the clearer they became.

If you loved your neighbor in the same way that you loved yourself, then you could simply not do anything offensive against him. That would take care of six of the commandments given to Moses about treatment of fellow humans. The first four commandments were covered in the simple statement to love God with every fiber of your being. If you truly did, you could not worship other Gods, could not utter blasphemies against God's name, could not swear vainly in His name, and would truly want to keep His Sabbath day holy, meditating on the goodness and the blessings of God. It was amazing to think how simple the teachings were, and yet how all-encompassing.

Whenever we were asked about exactly what being our neighbors meant, we all fell back on one of Jesus' famous stories about the Good Samaritan. It was a profound way of indicating that every human being on the face of the earth is our neighbor, whether we know their name or anything about them. All humans were made by God, and all are His children, therefore, we are all one large family as well. We have all been commissioned by God to love each other, care for each other, and protect and shelter each other. If all people did this, it would indeed be an ideal world.

One time when John had remained in Nazareth with Mary, I was traveling back from a stay in Antioch. I had been helping the members of the Way in their efforts to become true followers of Jesus, and continuing in the vein that had been started by Paul. I felt a strong call to return to Nazareth, to Mary's house, and was traveling in a small caravan when a messenger came by with a letter from John to me. When I identified myself as Mark bar Mathias, the messenger gave me the letter. Opening it, I read an urgent request from John. "Mary needs you to return as soon as possible. She has been given a very important task to do, and we all need you here to help us." I wondered at this cryptic message, but knew that it had something to do with my already having begun the trip, feeling as strongly as I did that I was needed there.

As I arrived at the courtyard of Mary's house, Mary of Magdala rushed out to greet me. She told me, "Mary has been acting strange lately, and I am sure that she has received many messages from Jesus. Please talk to her and find out what it is she has to do." I refreshed myself as well as I could, and entered the home to greet Mary.

She was seated before a loom, weaving, and I was again startled by her beauty. Even though she was getting advanced in age, she seemed to project this beauty from somewhere in her inmost being. She looked up at me, and rested her eyes on me for an instant, then stood up and rushed to me with outstretched arms. We embraced, and I felt again that she was my true mother. She wanted to hear all about my trip and everything that had transpired while I was away. John listened to my stories with eager interest, as did Mary Magdalene. Others in the house hastened to prepare a meal for us, and I felt that I had truly come home. I could feel the presence of Jesus in this house as though he was reclining at the table with us, as we shared some bread, cheese, fish, grapes, and wine.

After the meal, we went out to the courtyard to soak up the evening breeze. I wanted to ask Mary what was so urgent, but held myself back, knowing that she would speak in her own good time. We nibbled on some fresh fruit as we enjoyed the quiet and the coolness. Finally Mary turned to me and said, "Mark, I have been given an assignment by God, and He wants you to help me if you will accept His charge." I was astounded. God was asking me for my permission to accept His assignment? I never failed to be awed by the fact that God had given all of us free will, to make our own choices, and do what we wanted to do and go where we wanted to go. With His unlimited powers, He still allowed us the privilege of making our decisions, whether good or bad. Eagerly, I told Mary that I would be honored to help in whatever obligation God had asked of her.

Mary reminded me of the sacred objects that she had shown us long ago, so many of the things that Jesus had used, other things that had been associated with him during his last few days on earth, and his burial. I relived the emotions of seeing those objects as I acknowledged that I certainly did remember them. She then said, "Well, God wants all these things associated with His son to be taken to a special place. Somewhere that no one will be able to find them, not until the last days when they will be revealed to one who will be a trusted servant of God."

"Where in the world is there such a place?" I questioned. She answered, "I know fairly well where it is already, but you will simply need to follow my directions until we get closer to the place. I must pledge you and all who accompany us to the utmost secrecy." As it turned out, the people in our small party were, in addition to myself; John, Mary and her brother, Cleophas, Mary Magdalene, and Joseph, the man from Arimathea, in whose tomb Jesus had lain for those days after his death. Joseph had become one of our strongest allies after Jesus' resurrection. He had debated several times with Jesus and had come to believe that his teachings were the best blueprint for life itself. He had asked to be baptized, and this had been done by Peter. Joseph was fairly wealthy, and used much of his wealth to help the poor and the widows and orphans, as Jesus had instructed.

I made arrangements for our small group to travel with a larger caravan. I cannot write down so much as a direction that we went, in order to help protect the secrecy of what we were about to do. All I can relate is that we eventually found a caravan going in the right direction, and we joined with it. There was more safety in greater numbers, and even though I was still prepared to do battle to the death to protect Mary, it was far more prudent to avoid all possible trouble. I arranged for all the pack animals that we would need, and we all made preparations to depart. Mary had packed the sacred items in blankets and baskets, to make them look like things that she would be selling in a bazaar somewhere. All in all, we looked like an innocent group that had nothing to hide.

We traveled with the caravan for several days. When the caravan master came to our camp one night, we invited him to join us for our meal. He accepted gladly, and sat with us, regaling us with stories about some of his most exciting adventures in leading these caravans. We heard marvelous tales of all kinds, and thought this would certainly be an exciting life. As he arose to leave for the night, he mentioned that we would be turning in a new direction on the following day. Mary looked up and told him that we would be splitting from his group then, because we were going to visit some family and needed to go toward them. When he asked exactly where we were going, Mary said, "We were told to go to a certain place, and our family will meet us there to take us to our destination." He seemed satisfied by this answer and left.

We questioned Mary avidly about this dissemination. She said she had told only the truth, without divulging our goal or our aim. "God is our father, and Jesus is our brother. They are our family. They have already told me to go to a certain place, and it will be there that we will receive our final instructions, because at this time, I do not know what our final destination is either." As we discussed this amongst ourselves, we realized that God had given Mary specific instructions, but only as she needed to know, so that she could not lie about her destination, and it would help protect the location as well.

Next morning, as the caravan headed in one direction, our little group with our pack animals went in a different direction. After the caravan was completely out of sight, we changed directions yet again, and traveled over some very difficult terrain. We went through wadis and dried creek beds, over rough hills and through wooded and lush undergrowth. After more days of this rough travel, we found ourselves in some very strange country, with steep cliffs and jutting hills. Each day it seemed that Mary became more and more withdrawn, as though she was in constant communication with someone that only she could see and hear. She even seemed startled at times when one of us would speak to her.

At last we came to a place where there was a small spring for water. It was so well hidden that I didn't think anyone even knew of its existence. We rested for a few hours in the shade by the spring. Following the midday meal, Mary came to me and said, "This is the time. I have been told that only you and John are to go with me. The rest are to stay here until you return. Bring the pack animal with the holy relics with us." Consequently, we told the rest of our party to remain where they were, and we would be back as soon as possible.

The three of us trudged up one hill and through canyons with steep sides, where I worried about our vulnerability. Mary noticed my apprehension, and she placed her hand on my arm. "Do not worry, Mark, because we are totally under God's protection now. There is absolutely no thing or no one that can do us any harm now." This was reassuring to me, but I still caught myself watching for signs of an ambush.

As the sun began its' downward sweep toward the horizon, we arrived at a hill covered with brush. As I looked at the face of this hill, I saw an opening in the side, large enough for a person to walk into very easily. Mary saw it too, and she explained to us, "Mark, John, my sons, this is the place God has brought us to. It is the sacred resting place of the Ark of the Covenant, placed here by the prophet Jeremiah to protect it from desecration by the Babylonians. God has ordered that only I will be allowed to enter the place, for if you tried, you would probably be killed. Therefore, I will need you to unload all the items, and I will carry them in by myself."

Mary took first the burial shroud that wrapped the body of Jesus. As she entered the cave, we could hear a low, humming sound, and we felt the hairs on our bodies rising again. Mary returned with her face glowing, and carried the lance and the crown of thorns in next. She continued until she had every object safely placed within the cave in the hill. As she came out for the last time, she said, "Now I must bid you both farewell, for God is calling me home. I have fulfilled all the obligations that God has given me, and I give you my blessing. Please do not come near me, but know that I love you with all my heart." She took two steps forward, and looked up into the heavens. She folded her hands across her breast and her face became so radiant, that we could scarcely bear to look at her. A glow seemed to come from within her body, and spread outward, until she was completely surrounded in light. We could hear vaguely what sounded like beautiful singing, and then a cloud came from the skies and swirled around Mary. Her eyes widened, a beautiful smile crossed her face, and she said, "My son!" She stretched out her arms, and the cloud completely enveloped her. Then, she was gone! She simply vanished!

John and I had our eyes on her constantly, and knew that she was nowhere to be found on this earth. We looked at the opening of the cave, where Mary had stored the treasures, and it had closed completely. There was no trace of where it had been. We were sad and happy at the same time. Sad because we would miss our mother dreadfully, but happy that she had been reunited with her son, Jesus. We stayed in that place for a little while, and talked solemnly about all that we had seen. We knelt and prayed to God in thanksgiving for sharing his mother with us for so long, and felt her presence in our midst, even though she was no longer physically present.

Finally, we decided that we should return to the rest of the group, and we must hurry if we were to get there before full dark. We led the pack animal back through the steep hills and forbidding territory, which now seemed even more threatening than when we had first gone there with Mary. The sun set, and we were just able to see in the distance a little campfire showing where the rest of our group was.

Of course, as we came into the little campsite, everyone questioned us at once. "Where is Mary?" "Where have you been for so long?" Did something happen to Mary?" We raised our hands to quiet everyone and tried to explain exactly what had happened. Since most in our party had been present at the time when Jesus ascended into the heavens, they could easily believe what we were telling them. Joseph had not been there, and we described in more detail all the events that took place, and how Mary bid us all a very loving farewell. He accepted our story, but with amazement. No one had ever gone up to heaven without having died and being buried, not since the prophet Elijah.

We ate our evening meal without much conversation. Everyone was lost in their own thoughts and feelings, and all of us missed that gentle, loving presence in our midst. During the night, at times we all woke and continued to think our private thoughts, and turned to prayer for comfort. Next day, we began the long journey back to Nazareth. We must have still been under God's special protection, because we did not encounter any thieves or looters. We had no problems of any kind, and after many days of travel, we arrived again at Mary's house.

It gave all of us a sudden pang of sorrow when we entered the house, and Mary was not there. We desperately missed her quiet presence, her gentle voice, and her enduring love for all of us. I realized that we would only be able to see her once again when we rejoined her and Jesus in heaven, yet, her spirit seemed to be surrounding us constantly, especially in this house where she had spent so many years. We could also feel Jesus amongst us more strongly, since he, too, had lived in this house for a long time. We spent several days discussing what we were to do next, and it was during one of these nights that I had a very vivid dream.

In my dream, Jesus was walking toward me, as I was languishing in a prison somewhere, in chains. I watched him come nearer, and when he was standing directly in front of me, he stopped. I was lying propped up on the wall behind me, and tried to move to a position where I could prostrate myself before him. He reached his hand to me and touched the chains, and they broke and shattered and fell to the floor. Then he took my hand and helped me to my feet. He said simply, "Follow me!" and walked out the door. Of course I followed, and when we were outside the prison, he said, "Now you are totally free, and I have come to give you the specific instructions that I have promised to you."

I pledged that I would follow any instructions he had for me, and he proceeded to tell me what he wanted me to do. He told me that I was to continue to be his Gentile apostle, but was to be allowed more freedom to preach and help convert the Gentiles. Since I myself was a Gentile, he told me that other Gentiles would be able to relate to me and to the story I could tell them about my own conversion. He told me not to worry about confessing my former life as a Roman soldier, since his protection would surround me, and I would not be arrested by any Roman. Again, he promised that John and I would not die in his service, even though all the other apostles would be called to be martyrs. He said we would experience imprisonment and sometimes harsh treatment, but he said that we would live long and very fruitful lives.

We were to work feverishly to save as many souls as we could.

As soon as I agreed to do his will, Jesus embraced me, and I felt the most beautiful warmth and love welling up from the depths of my soul. I felt peace such as I had never before experienced, and I wanted to remain in his embrace forever. Sadly, though, he whispered to me, "Peace be with you, my peace I leave with you." And he was gone. I sat up suddenly, instantly awake from deep sleep, and I could still hear the swirling echoes of that last whisper weaving through the air around my ears. I immediately knew that this was a direct visitation from Jesus himself, and so reinforced my determination to do all that he had told me he wished for me.

I could not return to sleep, so quietly went outside to the courtyard. The sky in the east was just beginning to glow dimly, indicating that within an hour the sun would begin to rise. I smelled the heady aroma of blooming flowers, mingled with the scent of figs and grapes, delicately wafting through the pre-dawn air. I sat and contemplated all that Jesus had told me in my dream, and looked at the sky, pierced in thousands of places with the brightness of the stars. I prayed to God to be with me and give me strength and knowledge for the years ahead of me.

Soon, as the chickens began to announce the beginning of a new day, I became aware of another presence in the courtyard. I looked up and saw John standing there, looking at me quizzically, almost as though he had been aware of my dream too. I was happy to see him, and needed desperately to talk over all that had happened during the night. He listened intently, and then said, "Your dream was very symbolic, as I am sure that you know when thinking about it. You were a prisoner of the Romans just as much as our people were and are. You were imprisoned in your own pagan culture, with all the gods and goddesses you were taught to revere. When you accepted Jesus into your heart and gave him your love, he freed you from that prison. He has shown you the way to the one true God, and he knows that Gentiles will believe a fellow Gentile much more easily than they will listen to one of us Jews. I can see now that you and I are destined to travel together and preach and convert as many Gentiles as possible to follow Jesus.

"On the other hand, I can also see that you and I should be expecting to spend time here and there in various prisons. We have already been there before, and survived, and will be able to take anything that comes to us in the future. Jesus has told me that I will serve him for a long life on this earth, and will not suffer death in his cause. He told me the same thing about you, so I believe his leaving you with his peace is his way of giving you all the strength and courage that you will need during our work in the future. Jesus has spoken to me in dreams as well, and I know more about the work he has in mind for both of us."

It was startling to hear this interpretation of my dream from one that I had now come to think of as my brother. It was almost identical to the conclusions that I had drawn as I sat in the early morning thinking about what the dream meant. Now I was certain that it was more than just a dream, and John and I both decided that we would be working together as a team, and concentrate more on the Gentile peoples. As the rest of the household roused and began stirring, we went in to announce that we would be departing on our journey in just a matter of days.

Mark and John

John and I spent the next few days in Mary's house, making all the arrangements for what we believed would be our final journey. All of us talked about what Mary would want done with her house. Joseph discussed several possibilities with us, and we finally agreed that we would use the house for shelter for any needy widow with children, or anyone that needed help. Joseph gave Cleophas the charge of seeing to all this, and supplied him with the funds that he would need for the project.

Joseph and Mary Magdalene had determined that they would travel to spread the word of Jesus to all places that had not heard the good news. They would both preach and tell everyone of the need to repent and be baptized in order to save their souls and live forever in complete happiness with God in heaven. John and I chose to travel north and east of Palestine, while Joseph and Mary had plans to go to farther away places in the west than even Paul had reached. Mary was a riveting speaker, and every time that she began telling her story about Jesus, she drew an attentive listening audience. She seemed filled with the fire of the Holy Spirit, and had a magnetic quality that reminded me in a small way of Jesus himself. She and Joseph were dedicated to winning as many souls as possible, and soon the day came when we all bid each other farewell, thinking that it was very likely that we would never see one another in this world again.

When John and I reached Jerusalem, we met some of the apostles who were still staying around that area. We shared a feast on one of these evenings, and discussed what was happening to all of us. Some of the apostles seemed disappointed that Jesus had not returned as he had promised. When he had been taken to heaven in the clouds, I had also heard him promise that he would be with us to the end of time, and the angels had told us that he would return again to establish his kingdom on earth. John was one of the few who believed that it would be a very long time before Jesus returned. I knew that Jesus had engaged him in several intimate conversations, and so surmised that perhaps John had been given more information about Jesus' return than had the others.

John convinced the rest of the others that we just needed to be patient, and accept whatever happened to us in the name of Jesus. He even mentioned that Jesus himself had said that we would all suffer because of his name, but we must remain steadfast and strong. It didn't matter exactly when Jesus would return to this earth; we were all commissioned to labor unceasingly to convert souls to God. Thomas, as usual, was doubtful about John's views, but stated, "Well, I expected him to come long before now, so it can't be very much longer now. In the meantime, I am taking a group of people with me and traveling east along the Silk Road, to convert as many of those pagans as possible." Everyone was surprised at this announcement, but agreed that Thomas, as well as every one of us, had received a definite assignment from Jesus.

Some disciples wanted to remain in Palestine and work among the Jews. John and I informed them of our decision to work mainly among the Gentiles. Peter and Paul had already been laboring for years with the Gentiles as well as the Jewish people who had moved to outlying countries, and John and I wanted to follow them, and reach other countries to bring the good news to as well.

Before we left Palestine, I told John that I would like to see my father one last time. I had not seen him since I defected from the army, but had secretly found ways to know that he was still alive and how he was faring. I knew that he was now an old man, and I also knew that I would not see him again in this world. Therefore, John and I made arrangements to stop at my father's house where he was staying in Joppa, and we traveled there. We had to be very careful going in to the grounds surrounding his house, because there were Roman soldiers patrolling the streets, and they would challenge a couple of Jews that were attempting to enter a Roman citizen's home. We watched carefully for an hour or so to determine the pattern of their patrol, and when there was a brief period where we would be unnoticed, we slipped in through the gate and walked stealthily toward the house.

Soon the garden hid us from view of the main road, and we began to relax somewhat. We faced another challenge when we approached the door and a servant coldly asked us what our business was there. I remembered some of the Jewish businessmen that my father had traded with, and told the servant that I represented one of them, and really had need to see the master of the house. At this, the servant curtly told us to wait in the atrium, and went off to notify father that he had business guests.

My father slowly walked into the room. His hair was completely white, and he walked with a slight limp and his body seemed a little hunched over, but I could still tell that he was my father. Of course, he had never seen me with a full beard in the Jewish style, and dressed in that fashion, he seemed to have no clue as to my identity. I controlled myself as best I could until the servant was dismissed, and just the three of us were in the room.

I hesitantly began to speak to him, and at the sound of my voice, his head came up sharply and he peered intently at me. I said, "Father, it is I, Marcus, and I wished to let you know that I am all right, and wanted to see you once again to see how you are." As he studied me, I could see recognition slowly dawning on him, and he approached me trembling, with his arms outspread to embrace me. We fell on each other weeping and mumbling all sorts of incoherent thoughts. He told me that the authorities had notified him of my defection from the army, but since I had seemed to disappear from the face of the earth, everyone came to the conclusion that I had either fled the country or had been killed by bandits or someone else. He had given me up for dead.

We all sat down and father called for refreshments. When we were alone again, I introduced John to father, and began to tell him about all the events that led up to my total commitment to Jesus and his service. Light shone from father's face as I related all the wonderful things that I had experienced, and how I had been working with the other apostles to bring all the good news to everyone in the entire world.

After I finished my story, father told me what had been transpiring in his life. He told me that he had been following Jesus ever since my miraculous healing, and how he was convinced that Jesus had the power of God within him, in order to perform all the things he was doing. Father had gone to many of Jesus' lectures, and listening to his teachings led him to believe that Jesus had the truth that men always seemed to be striving to find. He ended with the simple statement that he and his entire household had been baptized by one of the apostles quite awhile after Jesus' death. All his servants had all accepted the teachings of Jesus and all had been baptized. There were some other Gentiles living in Palestine that were also converted to the Way, and they met at one another's homes to practice their faith as Jesus had taught.

Naturally, this made John and I very happy, and we stayed with my father for three days, talking constantly and reinforcing our faith in Jesus and his teachings. When I told father of the responsibility that Jesus had given to me, to be an apostle to the Gentiles, he understood, yet shook his head sadly. He knew that he and I would never see each other again in this life, yet we both now had hope of our eternal happiness with Jesus. Sadly, but with tender love, we bade one another farewell. John and I then left for what we believed to be our final journey.

Regardless of where we were traveling, there was always a group of people with us to help in our ministry. We gathered many disciples along the way, and when we found anyone with special talents that would be beneficial to our mission, we utilized those talents in our work. We had men who were proficient at handling money and were proven to be men of honesty and integrity. Those were put in charge of taking funds from converts, and spending for the benefit of all the needy in their area. There were many women as well. Some were happy doing the cooking and taking care of laundry and other mundane tasks that were necessary on our journeys. Others demonstrated an ability similar to that of Mary of Magdala, and would help us in preaching the word to people. Some women were actually left as deacons or elders to guide the churches that we established along the way. Any talent could be used in some way or another, whether it be a man or a woman. Some married couples were both left in charge of these fledgling churches.

We heard news from time to time about some of the other original apostles. When Gaius, otherwise known as Caligula, was selected Emperor shortly after Jesus' crucifixion, he was so cruel and unpopular, that he was murdered by one of his own guards in the fourth year of his reign. Claudius I was then seated on the throne, and things began to get touchy for Christians in the Roman provinces. We received many letters from Paul and Peter both, who at this time were living among the new Christians in Rome itself. They began to warn us of difficult times ahead when Nero became emperor.

Nero was very headstrong and somewhat eccentric. When a great part of Rome burned, he blamed the Christians in Rome for setting the fire, and began to seriously persecute anyone who professed the faith. Around this time, we heard that both Peter and Paul had been put to death. This caused us great sorrow, yet we knew that they were both receiving their rewards, which all of us were looking forward to eagerly. In the outlying provinces, we also heard of terrible persecutions of the Christians. Many were tortured and put to death for their belief. We continued to focus on Jesus' words, "Whoever is persecuted in my name, will have everlasting life." We needed these words to bolster our courage.

Meanwhile, back in Jerusalem, we heard that the Jewish zealots had begun a serious uprising against the Roman rule. The emperor Vespasian himself waged war on Jerusalem itself, and much to the dismay of all Jews, he razed the entire town, and completely destroyed the temple. About a thousand zealots retreated to the hilltop fortress of Masada, where they fought for over two years. Vespasian left to return to Rome and left his son Domitian to finish the siege of Masada. Eventually, the Romans did reach the top of the hill, only to find that the bulk of the fighters had committed suicide rather than once again submit to Roman rule.

All these events continued to sadden us as we received news from different parts of the world. John and I worked tirelessly to shore up the courage of our established communities, and to help the newer Christians in their belief that death was only the beginning of their eternal life, if they truly accepted Jesus.

At last, the dreaded day came when soldiers in Athens, where John and I were staying, arrested us. We prayed as they began rounding up many of our believers. Domitian was the Emperor at that time, and he seemed not as rabid as his predecessors had been in eradicating the Christians. When the soldiers arrested us, we were first put into a prison in chains, but later told that we were simply going to be banished.

This is how we arrived at the island of Patmos, with a few of our dedicated believers. We thanked God that our lives had been spared, but couldn't help feeling also a little sad. We had been preparing ourselves to face death and eternal life with Jesus, and being banished was totally different from what we had been expecting. After the ship dropped all of us on the island, we were completely cut off from all civilization everywhere. The island became our world. We couldn't communicate with anyone but one another, and we quickly set about making a new life for ourselves.

We had been given some livestock to take to the island with us, and since some people were already living there, there was an abundance of olives, grapes, and other crops. We soon realized that with some physical effort on our part, we could live in relative comfort, and without the constant fear of imprisonment and death. John was a natural leader, and I was used to being an organizer, so between the two of us, we set out duties for every one in our group. Some were commissioned to tend the livestock, others to cultivate and reap the crops, while yet others set about making shelters for everyone.

John and I found a cave halfway up one of the taller hills. From this vantage point, we could look out over the sea, and when the weather was very clear, catch a glimpse of one or more of the other islands scattered throughout the area. We made the cave into comfortable living quarters for us, and we traveled around the island speaking to the inhabitants there. None of them had ever heard of Jesus, and we found fertile soil there, both in the ground and in the minds of the people. Many of them were suspicious of us at first, but when they watched how we lived together and cared for one another, they began to realize that the Way was the best way to live life. Gradually, one after another asked for baptism, and soon the entire island was living their lives as Jesus desired.

We taught the people the same message we had repeated over and over again to everyone. That Jesus was truly the Son of the only God. That he had been mentioned countless times in the scriptures by all the prophets that God had sent. That he was born of a virgin, but had no earthly father, since God was his father, and his birth was miraculous. His entire life had been lived in humility and among the least of the people, and he loved them with a perfect love. He finally allowed himself to be tortured, ridiculed, and put to death on a cross in order to present the only perfect sacrifice to his father. That act brought salvation to the entire world, but everyone still had the free will to accept this wonderful gift.

For those who accepted the gift of God's salvation, and asked Jesus to come and live within their hearts, their lives would be forever changed, as ours had been. When we lived according to God's commandments and Jesus' teaching, our death would not be the end of us, but would be the beginning of an eternity of blissful life in heaven. John always preached the depth of God's love, how he had loved the world so much that he sent his only begotten son to die for us, so that we could have redemption for our sins and enjoy eternity in heaven with him.

The people accepted the story of Jesus' ultimate sacrifice, because everyone had been used to offering sacrifices to various gods throughout their entire life. The wonder of having received the perfect sacrifice to bring an end to the need for further sacrifices appealed to the people, and they saw the logic sometimes better than many people in some of the other countries that we had labored in.

Sometimes during the night, I would wake to find John standing at the cave opening, as if in a trance. If I spoke to him, he seemed not to hear. He later told me that he had been receiving visions from our dear Lord, and was instructed to write everything down. For many days he would sit at his writing table and write everything down that he saw in his visions. It was during this time that he told me that I should also write down the experiences that I had lived through getting to know Jesus.

Therefore, for weeks both John and I were like hermits, sleeping at night, receiving visions and writing everything down as we were instructed. After we both completed our tasks, we had some members of our group copy our words, so we would have more than one copy. It seemed as though John had known about our imminent release, because one day we saw a ship sailing toward our island, and it continued until it was close to shore. We watched as some smaller boats were rowed to the land, and we went down to meet them.

We were told that Domitian had died. The new Emperor Nerva and his adopted son Trajan had reviewed our case, decided that we were not a threat to the empire, and so decreed our release and freedom. Many of our little group had made this their home and did not want to leave. John and I felt that Jesus had led the Emperor to release us, but by this time, we were both old men ourselves. We packed up our few belongings, our writings, and bid a very melancholy farewell to those who wanted to stay.

Now we are free men once more. We have learned that every one of the original apostles had been put to death, just as Jesus had told both of us. We also realized that we had lived through all the imprisonments and persecutions, again, just as Jesus had told us. We decided to travel to Ephesus and finish out our years there, serving our saving Lord as well as we can, since we are both well advanced in years and not having the strength that we had as young men.

As I finish this story of my meetings with Jesus, the most important thing I can think of is that we must first love Jesus. In order to love someone, we must begin to know them as intimately as possible. This is how we will come to love Jesus, since all future generations will not be able to see him physically as I was blessed to. Read and study his words. Many of the later disciples have been keeping records of all that Jesus said and did. If these writings are truly from God, which I firmly believe, they will survive as long as it takes for Jesus to return again, as he promised. When I look back over my own experiences, I realize that I came to know Jesus gradually, and once I was totally committed to him, knew that this is a permanent commitment, just as a very close friendship with someone should be.

John told me that the book he had written on the island of Patmos was for all the future generations, as well as the main churches that had been established. He said that he could not even understand all that he had been shown, but had been instructed to write it down nevertheless. These words are supposed to be an indication of what will happen at the end of time, before Jesus comes again to reclaim his people. If people truly love Jesus, they will read these words with reverence, and be given some inspiration to understand them.

My own book is simply a chronicle of how I came to know Jesus, and by doing so, developed an all-consuming love for him. This love grew very gradually, and became more firm in my heart as I myself learned more about him. You also must learn about Jesus. Live your lives the way he taught us to. Love one another as he loved the entire human race. Keep your focus solely on him and his teachings. In this way, you will get to know him, and you cannot stop your overwhelming love for him as you get to know him better. Knowing him, loving him, and doing his will is the best guarantee for eternal happiness that I can think of, as well as the peace and joy you can experience in the world, even in the midst of persecution. If Jesus could take a rough, unfeeling pagan like me and turn me into what I am today, think of what great things he can do for you as well.

In the same way that I personally traveled some of the same paths that Jesus traveled, so will you as you learn about him. I have thanked the great God every day for sending his son to this earth for our salvation, and allowing me to be present to witness so many of the events of his life, death, and resurrection. You can experience these same things in your life if you truly set out to know him. The peace of our Lord and Savior, Jesus Christ, be with all of you reading my words.

CPSIA information can be obtained at www.ICGtesting.com
Printed in the USA
LVOW082355260313

326168LV00001B/10/A

9 781602 664753